LOTTIE - THE RUNAWAY

CATHARINE DOBBS
DOTTIE SINCLAIR

Copyright © 2025 by Catharine Dobbs & Dottie Sinclair

All rights reserved.

No part of this book may be reproduced in any form or by any electronic or mechanical means, including information storage and retrieval systems, without written permission from the author, except for the use of brief quotations in a book review.

PROLOGUE

1 865

LOTTIE WAS FREEZING. Her hands felt like they were made of ice, but she couldn't do anything about it. She had no gloves—she couldn't afford them—and her coat was so thin it was a surprise that it hadn't collapsed completely.

Even so, she tugged it around her thin body, buttoning up and turning the collar up, using her long hair to block the wind from going down her neck. It helped, but only a little bit. She adjusted her cap and stamped her feet and she wanted to go somewhere warm and hide away from everything. Lottie longed to sit beside a fire to get feeling back into her body; she couldn't feel her toes right now.

But she would be chased out. The last time she tried, she was told that she couldn't be there and was physically thrown out of the public house. That had been embarrassing, and Lottie couldn't look anyone in the eye afterwards. How could children be treated like that?

"Girl!"

Lottie jumped, almost dropping the broom she had been clutching. She turned and saw a tall, rather severe-looking woman looking down at her with a haughty expression in her eye. She wrinkled her nose at the sight of Lottie, jerking her head at the road.

"Clear the path for me," she ordered. "I don't want to have my skirts ruined by dung."

"Yes, ma'am."

Lottie gritted her teeth as she waited for a gap in between the coaches and carts that passed along the road before stepping onto the cobbles. There was a lot of activity along the street, both on the road and on the pavement, which made the place ideal if someone wanted to cross the road and needed a crossing sweeper. Especially when horses did their business in the street and nobody bothered to clean it up. Nobody wanted to walk around with horse dung clutching onto their shoes and clothes.

Lottie didn't have an option. She had to smell like she had been in a stable for most of her life doing this. But it paid something, even if it was miniscule.

Anything to get what she could for her and her brother.

She swept furiously and quickly, moving across the street while dodging the carriages that passed by, and the cabs driven erratically by men who shouted at her to get out of the road. Doing her best to ignore them, Lottie finished her task and hopped onto the opposite pavement. It was clear despite cartwheels crossing, but it wouldn't last long.

"Come across, ma'am!" she called.

The woman stepped off the pavement and strode across the road, walking with a confident stride and her head held high. Lottie observed her as she approached. She had to be middle-aged, possibly in her forties, with iron-grey hair pinned severely away from her face and kept tucked under a bonnet. She wondered who this woman was and what she did to command such a presence. There was something about her that made Lottie want to straighten up.

"Not bad," the woman remarked as she stepped onto the pavement. She dug into her pocket and brought out a money bag that clinked as it moved. "You'll do well today, young lady. With it nearing Christmas, you're going to get a lot of people who want to cross."

"I hope so, ma'am."

She looked Lottie up and down again, making Lottie feel like she was a piece of meat hung up in the butcher's shop.

"How old are you, girl?" the woman asked.

"I'm ten."

"And you're here alone?"

Lottie bit her lip and nodded. She hoped that she wouldn't be asked any further questions. She didn't want to get upset talking about her parents. It would just result in pity that she didn't need. All she wanted to do was get as much money as she could so she could go home.

"Well, make sure you're back before dark, little one." The woman got a penny out of her purse and dropped it into Lottie's outstretched hand. "It's very dangerous once it starts getting dark."

"I'll be long gone before then," Lottie said, shoving the penny into her pocket.

The woman's expression softened, and she nodded.

"Good."

It was not often that she had someone showing her a bit of kindness, even if it was brief. Lottie was certainly not used to it. It made her legs weak, and she could feel herself trembling.

Maybe she should use that to her advantage. She pretended to collapse, falling to the ground with a cry.

"Oh, my goodness!" The woman leaned over and reached for her. "Are you all right?"

"I'm fine." Lottie managed a smile as she was helped back to her feet. "It's just been a long day."

"When did you last eat?"

Lottie genuinely tried to remember, but she couldn't.

"Yesterday? I think?"

The woman looked horrified.

"What? You've not eaten in more than a day?"

"Can't afford it, ma'am."

That was true enough, and Lottie had another reason, but she wasn't going to reveal it. Otherwise, she was going to start saying everything, and she couldn't rely on anyone. Certainly not someone showing her a little kindness.

"Oh, you poor lamb." The woman pressed half a crown into Lottie's hand. "Use that to get you something decent to eat. And use it wisely."

"Thank you, ma'am." Lottie managed a small smile. "I will."

The woman touched her hand to Lottie's head before turning away abruptly and walking away. Lottie smirked to herself and looked at the purse she had snagged in the commotion. The woman had been so focused on Lottie's collapse that she hadn't noticed her purse had been taken. She might notice in a few minutes or not until she got home. Either way, Lottie knew she would need to make herself scarce before she was caught.

It would be enough to get something to eat before she went home. It would be what she needed, especially at this time of year.

Would it be a good idea to get a little treat for Billy? Would she have enough?

Lottie pushed that away. She would think about that later.

Looking around, she began to carry her broom with her along the street. She could get more money sweeping along here with the amount of people around, but if she was caught with someone else's purse on her, she would have to run. Lottie needed the street to be mostly clear so she could have a clear run and not have the fear of being grabbed and held for the constable.

As she neared the end of the road, sure enough, a constable turned into the road and began to walk towards her. Lottie slowed, her heart beginning to race even more. She did her best to avoid the police, but they seemed to be everywhere. Thankfully, most of them were not healthy when it came to running, and she could easily outpace them.

But it would just take one misstep, and she would end up being caught.

Holding her breath and trying to act normal, Lottie began to walk past him.

"You there! Stop!"

Lottie's heart almost stopped when she heard a familiar voice shouting. She turned and saw the woman she had just stolen from standing in the middle of the pavement, pointing directly at her in outrage.

"Stop that girl! She's just stolen from me!" she cried. "Give me back my money, you little brat!"

Everyone was stopping to look at her, and Lottie could feel herself panicking. She was within reach of the constable, who was now turning to look at her. His eyes narrowed, and he started to reach for her. Lottie darted out of the way, throwing the broom at him, and then broke off in a run.

"Get back here!" she heard a bellow. "Thief! Stop that thief!"

Then there was the loud sound of the constable whistle. It always made her ears hurt, and Lottie resisted the urge to clamp her hands over her ears. She kept running, dodging around crowds and into the road. She slipped on the horse dung, ending up on her hands and knees in the muck. But she scrambled up and kept going, pumping her arms in the hopes it would make her go faster.

The sounds of shouting roared in her ears, and she could hear the clattering of horses around her. More shouting, screams, and banging filled her head. But Lottie couldn't stop. If she did, she would end up in the courtroom and jailed for theft. The prison system didn't care if it was a child that had committed a crime; they had to be punished.

She couldn't afford to let that happen.

CHAPTER 1

Lottie's chest was in agony, and she could hardly breathe as she ran down one alleyway, and then another. She could hear the shouting for the thief, but it was getting further away. Had they lost her?

She hoped so. She couldn't keep running much longer.

Her legs were hurting, and Lottie stumbled into the next alley. There was a small alcove off to the right, and she tucked herself into the space. If she stayed still and in the growing shadows as dusk fell, she wouldn't be seen. She would just have to wait.

She held her breath as she listened, wondering if the voices and running feet were getting closer. She couldn't hear anything, but that didn't mean anything. It could be a false sense of security. Knowing her luck, she would leave her hiding spot and walk straight into him.

After a while, Lottie heard nothing but silence. Either the ringing in her ears was worse, or she had managed to give the law the slip. She hoped it was the latter.

Billy couldn't afford for her to be arrested. Not now.

Lottie counted slowly to ten, and then again, and then for a third time. When she didn't hear anything after that, she stepped out of her hiding place. It wasn't far from her destination, but she had to take it slowly. If anyone recognised her and realised she was a thief, the chase would start again.

And she was very thirsty. Her mouth was dry. She needed to get something to drink.

It wasn't long before she ended up alongside the river. The murky-looking water swirled below her, and it made Lottie feel nauseous. She was almost thirsty enough to dunk her cupped hands into the disgusting mess, but not quite. She didn't want to get sick as well.

"Lottie?"

Lottie jumped and turned. Mrs Rush, one of the washerwomen, was watching her nearby. Lottie managed a smile as if she hadn't just been running away from the police.

"Good afternoon, Mrs Rush," she called. "Are you well?"

"As well as can be expected on a day like this." Mrs Rush peered at her. "What have you been up to?"

"What do you mean?"

"Your face is flushed, and you're breathing heavily." The woman narrowed her eyes. "You haven't been getting into trouble again, have you?"

"Me?" Lottie tried to look innocent, pointing at herself. "I'm never getting into trouble, Mrs Rush."

The washerwoman didn't look as if she believed her, pursing her lips with a sceptical expression. Lottie wasn't about to tell her what she had been up to. For one thing, Mrs Rush was incredibly nosy, and she would want to help as much as she could, and Lottie found her overbearing. And for another, she was a gossip, and Lottie didn't want her problems spread across the rest of the washerwomen as they cleaned clothes.

Her mother might have worked with them, but she wasn't about to give them something to talk about.

"I'm just going to Billy," she said brightly, walking on wobbly legs in the opposite direction. "He's probably back from school now."

"Are you sure he should be going to school, Lottie? He looked rather pale when I saw him earlier."

"He's fine," Lottie called back. "It's just this time of year. He doesn't do well with the cold."

Mrs Rush sighed.

"All right, but if things are a struggle right now, just let us know. You know we would help Elizabeth's children."

Lottie simply waved a hand over her shoulder to indicate she had heard. Everyone was aware that Elizabeth and Michael Watson had passed away and left their two young children behind, but they didn't know that it was Lottie looking after them on her own. She had claimed her Aunt Emily came by every day to look after them. That was partly true; her mother's sister did come to see how they were, but she did it twice a week and barely stayed more than a couple of minutes. It was like she was uncomfortable being in the squalor that Lottie and Billy had to call their house.

She did give money to them, but it was not enough to live on until Aunt Emily came back to see them. Lottie supposed that her aunt was paying for their rent to stay there as she didn't want to take them in, but it didn't make her, and Billy feel wanted. They had just been discarded.

Lottie hated feeling like she was a burden, but what could she do? Nobody listened to a child.

She reached her home, the tiny, terraced house at the end of the row, and let herself in.

"Hello?" she called, seeing her breath in the air. "Billy?"

"I'm here."

His small voice came from the back room. Lottie found him sitting huddled beside the fire, which was roaring away, a blanket around his shoulders. He was shivering despite the warmth in the room, sitting as close to the fire as he could without setting himself on fire. Lottie wanted to hug him, assure him things were going to be fine.

She managed a smile and walked towards him.

"How are you feeling?" she asked, kissing his head before settling on the floor beside him. "Was school all right?"

"I didn't feel very well halfway through," Billy mumbled, his chin barely above the blanket. "I asked if I could go home, and they didn't let me. I felt sick on the way home, and I've stayed here ever since."

"You didn't hurt yourself building and lighting the fire, did you?"

Her brother rolled his eyes.

"I'm nine years old, Lottie. I'm nearly ten. You were lighting fires when you were younger than me."

"Sorry, I'm…"

Lottie didn't know what to say to that. She knew that Billy was growing up, but it was hard to imagine him more than the chubby little toddler who had followed her around everywhere. Even though there was barely eighteen months between them, her brother was standing to match her in height. It wouldn't be long before he grew taller than her.

He would be just like Pa.

Lottie didn't want to think about that. She held up the purse and jangled the money inside.

"Look what I got," she declared.

Billy frowned.

"You stole again, didn't you?"

Lottie sighed and lowered the purse.

"We've got to do something, Billy! And if we need money for the doctor…"

"I'm sure I'll be fine in the next few days."

That was when Billy started coughing loudly, and it hurt her ears to hear that noise. It was so painful.

"Even so, I want you to get better."

LOTTIE - THE RUNAWAY

Billy shook his head.

"You worry too much, Lottie. We'll be fine." His hand moved under the blanket, and Lottie realised he was rubbing his stomach. "I feel sick, but I'm really hungry as well."

Lottie could understand that, although she had gone without for some time, so it was easier for her to ignore the hunger pangs. She managed a smile, which was shaky.

"I'll go and buy something. Then we can cook dinner. Is there anything you want in particular?"

"Whatever we can get." Billy swallowed. "I'm so cold."

Lottie felt tears pricking at her eyes, and she blinked them back. She wasn't going to get upset seeing her little brother like this. It just made her feel more worthless.

She didn't need that right now.

* * *

BILLY LAY HUDDLED in his blanket by the fire, curled in a ball with his eyes closed. He had fallen asleep almost immediately after their meal, leaving Lottie to clear everything up. His breathing didn't sound good, almost like a rattling noise.

It was horrible to hear.

After cleaning up, Lottie went over to the window and sat down, watching the world go by. People were leaving work and going back to their homes, ready to eat and fall asleep before doing the same thing the next day. That was how life was where she lived: everything was the same. It was boring and predictable.

But they didn't have much of an option. Their parents were dead, their aunt didn't want them, and Lottie couldn't get any work beyond the simple, tiny jobs that were incredibly boring and barely paid at all.

They were stuck, and Lottie hated it.

It wasn't anyone's fault. Nobody expected Ma and Pa to die when they did. There was something called a cholera outbreak going on, and they had made sure Lottie and Billy didn't drink dirty water. They warned them about what could happen if they did so. But that didn't stop them from drinking it, anyway, and then both took ill. Pa pulled through, but Ma didn't, and she died almost a week after she had to take to her bed. Pa carried on as best he could, trying to bring money in for his children, but he worked so hard that he was exhausted, and he collapsed at work, unable to get back up again. The doctor had said his heart had just stopped, unable to carry on any longer.

Lottie still remembered both of those days. It had left her in shock. Her parents had been strong and healthy all her life, and she never saw them sick. To see this happen so fast had left her reeling, especially when she was told that her father was dead as well. His last pay packet went towards a simple funeral for him.

Now it was just her and Billy, Lottie having to leave school so she could find work and do whatever she could to keep her and Billy out of the orphanage. People said that would be the best option for them, but Lottie knew they would have a worse life there. The stories she had heard about the workhouse were terrifying, and she didn't want anything to do with it.

They were going to continue as they were. Things would get better. It would get to a point where Lottie wouldn't need to steal so they could survive. They would be able to cope. She was confident about that. Once Billy got better, they would be able to get more money coming in. They weren't helpless.

She was scared, though. Billy had been getting sicker, and it was a wonder he was standing upright. If he didn't get better, she was going to lose him as well. But they didn't have the money for a doctor. Lottie knew she couldn't afford it, even if she went and stole several purses in one afternoon.

She would have to talk to her aunt about it. But would Aunt Emily be charitable enough to do that for them? She seemed to see Billy and Lottie as a burden. She refused to let them come into her home, saying that she didn't have the room. It was nothing short of a miracle that she was even coming by to make sure they were still alive.

Lottie leaned her head against the glass, watching her breath form on the glass. She would have to ask her aunt about it. With Billy as sick as he was, they couldn't stay here. He needed medical attention.

Even if she took just Billy, Lottie would be happy enough with that. She couldn't let it happen any further. She couldn't afford to lose her brother, too.

That really would break her heart.

CHAPTER 2

"I'm sorry, Lottie, but I can't take him in," Aunt Emily said.

Lottie stared at her like she had gone mad. Had she really said that?

"But why?" she protested. "Billy's ill!"

"We haven't got the room for him. You know that." Aunt Emily sounded impatient. "Stop asking for something you know you're not going to get and consider yourself grateful that I'm even checking on you."

Lottie wanted to scream at her, but how was that going to help. It would likely send her aunt walking the other way. She blinked back the tears in her eyes.

"Please?" she begged quietly. "If you can't, at least help us pay for a doctor."

"Why should I?"

"Because he's sick! He needs someone to help him."

Aunt Emily stood in the doorway, looking over at Billy as he lay on the settee, wrapped in whatever blankets Lottie had managed to find. He was coughing, his face pale and streaked with sweat. Lottie flinched each time he coughed. It sounded painful.

"Well, there's not much I can do about it, Lottie," Aunt Emily said, although her expression said she didn't care. "I can't afford that on top of your bills."

"But..."

"No 'buts' about it. You may be my sister's children, but I said I'd make sure you two stayed in your home. I never said anything about paying for anything beyond your rent, and you should consider yourself lucky that I'm doing that."

Lottie's chest was tightening. She could hardly breathe. How could her aunt be so cruel? Didn't she know that Billy could die if he didn't get anyone to see him?

"Then what am I supposed to do?" she demanded. "I can't do this on my own! Billy needs help! I don't want my brother to die." Tears were beginning to fall down her cheeks, and she didn't care that the woman standing before her could see. "Please, Aunt Emily. Please help us."

Aunt Emily's eyes narrowed. She clearly looked annoyed about having to deal with this. Lottie couldn't understand how someone could be this way about family. Certainly, her aunt had married well and had a better lifestyle, but she couldn't throw her niece and nephew aside, could she?

"You're desperate, are you?" Aunt Emily asked finally.

"I don't want to be, but yes." Lottie nodded. "I want my brother to get better."

"Then get him up. I'll have a cart sent for you."

"From whom? Are we going to get a doctor?"

Aunt Emily just nodded once and turned away.

"When the cart driver arrives, get on the cart and you'll be taken to where you need to go. I'll sort out payment for his time."

"Thank you, Aunt Emily," Lottie said fervently. "I appreciate this."

The woman didn't respond, disappearing. Slightly elevated

knowing that she could get her brother some help, Lottie hurried over to the settee and gently shook Billy.

"Wake up, Billy," she whispered. "We're going to see the doctor."

"What?" Billy blinked his eyes open, his voice hoarse. "Are we? But I thought Aunt Emily…"

"She's going to help us. I just need you to get up." Lottie tugged at his arm. "Come on, quickly! They're not going to wait for us."

It took longer than she thought to get her brother onto his feet, but once he was moving it was easier to get him out of the house. Lottie held onto him, hoping that he didn't collapse on her. Billy was thin and frail, but she was still not strong enough to hold him up. She was worried that his bones would snap if she tugged too hard.

They hovered on the doorstep in the biting cold, the wind whipping around them, and then a cart came around the corner. A gnarly looking man with a bald head and a scowl on his unshaven face was sitting up the front. He stopped in front of the house and glowered at the siblings.

"You are needing a ride somewhere?" he growled.

"Yes, please." Lottie led Billy to the back of the cart and heaved him on board. "Aunt Emily paid you, didn't she?"

"She did. Something about getting you to where you belong."

"Yes." Lottie pulled herself onto the cart and scrambled to the front. "Where's the nearest doctor?"

He didn't answer. Instead, he flicked the reins, and the horse pulled away, almost knocking Lottie off-balance so she had to grab onto the side of the cart. She shifted back to Billy, who was still curled up in blankets. His forehead was hot to the touch as she stroked his head.

"It's going to be all right," she whispered. "You'll be better soon."

But it didn't take long before she realised that they weren't going in the direction she thought they would go. From her recollection, the doctor they normally used lived in the opposite direction. The driver was taking them east, away from the places Lottie recognised and into an area she had never ventured into. She looked around.

"Excuse me?" she called. "Where are we going?"

"We're going to get you help," he replied, not turning around. "You wanted help, didn't you?"

"I did, but…"

"Then sit down and shut up. I'm not paid to talk to you."

Lottie didn't like where this was going. It was beginning to feel disconcerting. If she was on her own, she would have jumped off the cart and run away. But Billy was with her, and he was in no fit state to run anywhere. She had to stay with him.

They were stuck, and she had no idea where they were going.

She felt a sinking feeling in her chest when they reached a huge, blank-looking building that towered beyond a high wall. The gates were open, and the driver led the cart through. Lottie caught sight of the sign on the wall before it was gone.

Orphanage and Workhouse. East End.

"What?" She sat up. "We're going to the orphanage?"

"You'll get help there."

"But I told Aunt Emily that we needed a doctor!" Lottie cried. "We don't need to be here!"

The driver looked at her with a slight sneer that made Lottie feel fear ripple down her back.

"She said that you two needed to be put where you would be dealt with, that she wasn't going to listen to your whining any longer. It was her idea to put you here."

"No," Lottie croaked. She couldn't believe it. "She wouldn't do that."

"Well, she did. She was clearly fed up with looking after a pair of orphaned brats. She paid me handsomely to get rid of you." The driver shrugged. "Consider yourself lucky. I could've taken you elsewhere that would make you two more useful than being stuck in the orphanage."

Lottie's panic was rising. This was what they had been trying to avoid. Her parents hadn't wanted either of them to go there, wanting their children to stay with family. Aunt Emily had promised to look after them, but then she did it at arm's length. Now she had discarded them.

How could she?

The cart stopped outside the main doors, which opened a moment later as Lottie huddled next to her brother. She watched as a tall, lean man with raven-black hair in a widow's peak strolled towards them. He nodded at the driver.

"Good day. To what do we owe this visit?"

"I've got a couple of orphans in the back." The driver jerked a thumb over his shoulder. "Their aunt didn't want to take care of them anymore."

"I see." The newcomer gave Lottie a smile. "Hello, little girl. What's your name?"

"We're not going in there," Lottie said tightly, glaring at him.

"I'm afraid you don't have a choice. You've been brought here, and you're going to have to come in. This is where children with no parents come, after all."

His voice was gentle, but there was a hard edge to him. Lottie could see it in the gleam in his eyes. She didn't like him at all. Her gut was saying he was a bad man.

They needed to get out of here. She looked around, trying to find anything that could help, but there was nothing. They were trapped, and Lottie wasn't about to leave Billy behind.

"Your brother doesn't seem very well." The gentleman strolled around to the back of the cart, leaning in to peer at Billy. "He looks ill, in fact."

"He's sick," Lottie croaked. "We need a doctor."

"Well, we have a doctor inside. He can take care of him." The smile was turned back to her. "You don't have to worry about anything. We can look after him."

Lottie didn't believe that at all. Her heart was pounding, and she felt like she was going to be sick. She scowled at the man.

"We're not going in," she said defiantly.

Billy coughed hard, and the sound made Lottie's stomach retch. It was horrible to hear. The gentleman sighed.

"Do you want your brother to die?" he asked. "Because that will happen if you keep dawdling around here."

"That's not fair!" Lottie cried.

"Just get her off the cart!" the driver snapped. "I want to get back to what I was doing, and those two are not helping."

Lottie wanted to kick at the gentleman as he reached for Billy, who barely reacted as he was pulled towards the edge of the cart. She didn't want him touching her brother. But if they had a doctor...

She had no choice. They had to go inside.

* * *

LOTTIE SAT by her brother's bed, listening to him croak as he slept. He had passed out as they brought him into the infirmary, and he was as pale as the sheets he was lying on. She wanted to cry at the sight of him, but she needed to stay strong. Someone had to remain strong with everything that was going on.

She couldn't believe her aunt had done this to them. If she hadn't ever wanted to take care of them, why didn't she just send them to the orphanage to begin with? Lottie didn't want to be here, but at least now she knew where she stood with the woman who promised to look after her and Billy as Ma lay dying.

Now they were here, and they weren't going anywhere until they were old enough to leave. If they were lucky, they might get a job in another factory somewhere in the city, or something of the like. That was the best option, but it wouldn't pay anything. And there was no guarantee that they would be able to leave together. They would end up being pulled apart, and Lottie was not about to let that happen.

She couldn't lose her brother.

"Lottie."

She looked up. The gentleman who had met them, who she now knew as Mr Fletcher, was standing at the end of the bed, hands clasped in front of him. She scowled at him.

"Go away."

"You're going to have to go to bed. It's late now."

"I'm staying with my brother. I can sleep in the next bed."

But Mr Fletcher shook his head.

"You're not sick, so you can't stay in here. You can go with the other children and sleep. There's a bed free for you."

Lottie didn't want to go anywhere, but she knew she didn't have a choice. She would be dragged there, just as she had been dragged into the orphanage earlier. Her arms were still throbbing from the fingers digging into her, and she was sure her skin was bruised. She had fought to remain with Billy as he was being taken care of, but that couldn't last forever.

"Will I be able to see Billy tomorrow morning?" she asked.

Mr Fletcher nodded.

"Of course. Now, you need to get some sleep."

She wanted to say she wasn't tired, but she found herself yawning. Smiling, Mr Fletcher stepped around to her side and placed a hand on her shoulder. Instantly, Lottie tensed. She didn't like that at all.

"Come on, sweetheart."

"Don't call me sweetheart," Lottie said tightly as she stood up. "I don't like it."

He held up his hands.

"Fair enough."

Leaning over, Lottie kissed her brother's forehead, which was cooler than it had been a few hours ago. At least he was starting to get through the worst. Then she was led from the room by Mr Fletcher. He kept a hand on her shoulder, and Lottie kept shrugging him off, only for his hand to go back to where it had been before.

She hated it.

They were at the foot of the stairs when there was a voice behind them calling out.

"Mr Fletcher?"

They turned. A short, buxom woman with fair hair walked towards them, dark circles under her eyes and pure exhaustion on her face. She frowned at Mr Fletcher.

"What are you doing?"

"I'm just taking Lottie up to her room," he replied, giving her a disarming smile that made Lottie shiver. "She's new, so she doesn't know where she's going, Amy."

Amy frowned at him in disapproval.

"You know you're not supposed to be anywhere near the girl's dormitory, Mr Fletcher. Mrs Cardle told you to stay with the boys."

"There's no one to take her."

"Well, I'm here now. I'll take her to her bed." Amy jerked her head. "Go and find something else to do."

Mr Fletcher's eyes narrowed, and Lottie felt his fingers dig into her shoulder. She flinched and pulled away from him, which made him let go. Clearing his throat, Mr Fletcher fixed a bland smile on Amy before walking away.

"I'm sorry about that," Amy said, turning to Lottie. "We've had the girls say Mr Fletcher makes them uncomfortable. There's very little we can do except put him elsewhere, but with how things are…"

"I don't want to be here," Lottie whispered. This time she didn't stop the tears. "I want to go home."

Amy sighed.

"I know you do. We all want to go home, but we haven't got one anymore. We must put up with what we've got."

"We were lied to! We shouldn't be here!"

Amy gave her a sympathetic smile and brushed Lottie's hair from her face.

"I'm afraid we can't do anything about that. You're here now, and things won't be that bad. You'll be able to find your way."

"What about my brother?" Lottie demanded. "Wherever we go, we'll go together, won't we?"

Amy hesitated before she answered, and Lottie didn't like that.

"We'll see. Shall we find you your bed? You must be exhausted. You look like you need some sleep yourself."

Lottie nodded. She wanted to sleep, but she wanted to be by Billy's side. She couldn't bear to be away from him, especially when things were like this. How could she protect him if she was elsewhere?

"Come with me." Amy stepped around her and headed up the stairs. "We're at the end of the hall. And we're going to have to be quiet. Some of these boards creak, and a lot of the children sleep lightly. I don't want to have to scold anyone tonight."

Lottie silently followed the woman upstairs and down the hallway, careful where she put her feet. There was a window at the end of the room, moonlight shining in and casting a silvery light across the floor. She glanced out and saw the yard outside. There was no garden. She could see some bushes and a couple of trees, but no grass. It looked as if there were plenty of workstations set up. Even in the cold, it looked as if they had been used quite a bit.

Did they force children to work outside in such weather? Lottie wanted to run away and beg to leave again, but she was getting too tired to argue.

Amy opened the door carefully and slowly, sticking her head into the room. Then she beckoned Lottie to follow her.

"This will be your bed," she whispered, pointing at the bottom bunk directly opposite. "We all have assigned beds, and that will be yours."

"Where will my brother sleep?" Lottie whispered back.

"He'll sleep with the boys in their dormitory. We keep boys and girls separated during the night."

"And I'll see him tomorrow?"

Amy gulped and her smile didn't reach her eyes.

"I'm sure you will. Now, get some sleep. You're going to need it."

She left, closing the door silently behind her, leaving Lottie in the darkness. There were windows along the opposite wall, but they had bars across them. Moonlight came in, but they didn't cast any light. Everything seemed to be shrouded in shadows.

It was eerie, and made Lottie want to run away. Instead, she went over to the remaining empty bunk, took off her shoes, and lay down under the blanket. The bed was hard and narrow, and the mattress was lumpy. She couldn't get comfortable for a long time.

But when she did finally fall asleep, she was thinking about how she could get out of here with her brother.

CHAPTER 3

1866

Lottie's hands were hurting. She hated doing this job, picking apart the rope into individual strands. Her nails were broken, and her fingertips were sore and bleeding. She wanted to stop, but she had already been told several times that she couldn't, and she would be caned if she stopped again.

Lottie was fed up with it. The backs of her legs were so sore from the caning that she was surprised she could move at all, much less sit down. But the people who watched over her were harsh. Sure, there were a few nice people—like Amy and the cook—but everyone else didn't seem to have a nice bone in their bodies.

Except Mr Fletcher. Lottie didn't know about him apart from the fact she was sure he was bad news. Some of the older girls had warned her about him the first breakfast after she arrived. He was a lecherous man who preyed on the girls for monetary value. Lottie wanted to know what he did but, at the same time, she didn't. She had a feeling she could guess, anyway.

She did her best to keep away from him in the weeks after

coming to the orphanage, but he always seemed to be lingering around, openly watching her. It was disconcerting.

"My fingers are stiff," Billy said as he flexed his fingers, wincing as he did. "I'm surprised they haven't snapped off."

"Same here." Lottie looked up at the sky, seeing the blossom on the trees. "At least the weather's improved and it's a little warmer out here."

"I wish we could be inside, though." Billy made a face. "I've never wanted to be in the schoolroom more than ever."

Lottie couldn't agree more. She was surprised that the orphans had school lessons at all, given everything going on in the building, but she was relieved that she could go back to them as well. The children were cut off from their lessons at the age of thirteen, and Lottie was not looking forward to that. She enjoyed learning. It was a reprieve from splitting rope into yarn, anyway.

She hated being here, but what could they do? Unless they were lucky and someone came by looking to adopt or to find workers, they weren't going anywhere. It was a miracle they went outside the orphanage to go to church. Lottie hadn't liked going to church in the beginning, but now she longed for those short hours sitting in the pews listening to the vicar droning on and on about something in the bible. It was boring, but better than what she had.

"Lottie! Billy!"

Amy was approaching them, her skirts billowing around her legs as she strode over. Lottie straightened up. Was this a chance to stop what they were doing?

"Yes?"

"We've got some paper from the paper mill that needs to be delivered to the printing press down the road, but we haven't got any day labourers available to take them. Could you and Billy…?"

Lottie and Billy were nodding almost before she finished speaking.

"Absolutely," Lottie said eagerly. "We can do that."

Anything to get out of the orphanage. Billy glanced at her, and she could see what was going through his head. Maybe this was their chance to escape? Amy sighed.

"Before you think you can run away, Mr Fletcher said he would be going with you."

Lottie deflated immediately.

"Oh."

"I told him that he has other duties to attend to, and I would take you instead." Amy gave them both a warning look. "So, behave yourselves, all right? I don't want to have any problems."

Both brother and sister nodded. Neither of them wanted to hurt Amy as they both liked her. She had the rare qualities of kindness and compassion, something that was hard to find now, and they wouldn't be able to hurt her.

Sighing, Amy turned away.

"Come along. The sooner we do this, the sooner we can get back to your usual duties."

"I'd rather not," Billy muttered, but they followed her around the side of the building and towards a cart, which was piled with paper. The paper mill nearby sent the stacks they made to the orphanage, and then they transferred it out to where it needed to go. The printing press was nearby, and so it wouldn't take long to hand it over.

It was a shame they couldn't go any further.

As they reached the cart and clambered onto it, Lottie looked back and saw Mr Fletcher watching them. His eyes were focused on her with a leer on his face, and it sent a shiver down her spine. Why was he so fixated on her? It was not nice, and Lottie knew if she brought it up to him he would play it off and say she was imagining things.

She had no idea why a man like him would work in an orphanage. It was strange, and he didn't belong, but nobody questioned his presence. It made her wonder what he was up to.

Amy led the cart out of the gates, and they made their way

down the street. The printing press was at the end of a long street, right near the river. Lottie had asked before why the paper mill didn't just send the paper straight to the printing press, but she had been told they had a deal with the paper mill, and it was money they needed. She didn't ask further after that.

It didn't take long to get there, and as Lottie and Billy began to unload the stacks off the cart and pile it up outside the squat building, a boy walked out. He was older than them, closer to maybe fifteen years of age, and slim, with dark hair curled tightly on his head. He looked fresh and clean as if he had washed that morning, and his clothes fitted well on his frame. Lottie felt a pang of envy seeing that. Someone was looked after while she and Billy were left to rot away.

He smiled at her, and Lottie was momentarily distracted. It was a very nice smile, one that made his blue eyes twinkle. Then he turned and addressed Amy.

"Thank you for this," he said. "Mr Pratchett said he would pay you later today once he's got things sorted here. It's very busy right now."

"Not a problem, Henry. We're happy to help." Amy glanced at Billy and Lottie. "Billy, I need to run some errands in the market. Would you mind helping me out?"

"Of course." Billy bounded over to her. "Where are we going?"

"Just to a few stalls. Cook wanted a few extra ingredients, so I must collect them while I'm at it." Amy raised her eyebrows at Lottie. "You stay here with the cart, Lottie. And don't do anything silly."

"I'll keep an eye on her, Amy," Henry said before Lottie could respond. "You don't need to worry about it."

Lottie glared at him, wishing he hadn't said that. She felt like she needed a guard for herself. Huffing, she went back to lifting the paper off the cart. At least she was out of the orphanage for a few minutes. She might as well make the most of it.

* * *

"Thank you for doing this," Henry said, coming out of the building again as Lottie climbed onto the back of the cart. "My employer does appreciate the help."

"It's something different for me to do." Lottie settled with her back against the side, tucking her skirt over her legs. She didn't want him to see the bruises. "Why don't you get it directly sent to you? Why come by us?"

Henry shrugged.

"I never asked. Mr Pratchett never told me about it, just that we have an arrangement. I just get on with what I'm told."

"You work here, then?"

"I'm an apprentice." Henry looped his arms over the side of the cart, resting his chin on his forearm. "I used to be at the orphanage myself until about eighteen months ago. Then I was taken in by Mr Pratchett, who was looking for an apprentice. I was more than eager to do something that wasn't random stuff at the orphanage that made me want to cause a riot."

Lottie couldn't help but smile at that.

"I can't argue with that. We're splitting rope so the sailors can plug up the holes in their boats."

"I wondered about the cuts on your hands. You would never think that rope could do that to you." Henry watched her curiously. "Do you mind if I ask you how long you've been there? I've not seen you and the lad around here before?"

Lottie was about to snap that it wasn't any of his business, but then she realised that she was being too mean. It was only a question, and Henry was showing some kindness to her. She might as well make the most of a friendly face.

"Since just before Christmas," she answered. "We—my brother and I—lost our parents about a year before, and our aunt was meant to be looking after us. But then she decided we were too much trouble and tricked us into going to the orphanage."

"Isn't that where you should have gone?"

Lottie snorted.

"We didn't want to go anywhere near it. She was paying rent for our home, and I was managing to look after us with what little money I could get. But Billy...he was sick..." She swallowed, still remembering how harrowing it had been. "She made me think we were going to the doctor, and she sent us to the orphanage. Billy recovered, but we've been stuck since."

Henry gave her a sympathetic look.

"Sounds like she never wanted to look after you."

"I hated her for that. I couldn't believe she could be so horrible as to do that to us."

"She didn't want to take you in?"

Lottie shook her head. She was feeling cold talking about it, feeling the rage at what Aunt Emily did to them.

"She claimed it was her husband who didn't want us around, but I think it was her who didn't care. Now she's gotten rid of us, and I bet she's happy to be saving money on our rent."

"I had something similar happen to me," Henry said quietly. "My mother died when I was six, and for six months my father looked after me. But then he started seeing a new woman who didn't like me. She manipulated him into sending me to the orphanage and forgetting about me."

"Oh, my goodness," Lottie breathed. "That's horrible."

"I spent years wondering what I'd done wrong. Why would he abandon me like that?" Henry shrugged. "But then I realise now that he was just more interested in having a wife than a son, and I was in the way. He can rot, for all I care."

"That's harsh."

"It's been nine years, and I'm still bitter about it. Things like that stay with you, Lottie."

Lottie couldn't argue with that. She knew what had happened to her was going to stay for a while, but would it ease off until she barely recalled it? Probably not. Not when she was stuck in a place like that.

Maybe this was a good time to ask more about Mr Fletcher and why he was there. Henry had to know about him. Perhaps she could figure out why a man like him was at the orphanage. But before she could say anything further, she heard Billy's voice calling her name. Sure enough, he and Amy were walking towards them, Amy carrying a basket full of food. Billy had a basket as well, and Lottie could tell he was resisting the urge to swing it as he walked.

"One moment." Henry pushed away from the cart. "Don't go anywhere."

"What?"

He disappeared inside, reappearing a moment later with something wrapped in a handkerchief. He held it out to her.

"Take it."

"What is it?"

"Sandwiches. They're for my lunch."

"What?" Lottie stared. "Your sandwiches?"

"I know how bad the food is there, and getting whatever you can is important." Henry smiled. "I'm just looking out for fellow orphans who are going through what I did."

Lottie didn't know what to say to that, but her stomach did the talking for her, growling at the thought of having more food. Henry's smile warmed.

"I can manage without a meal now, but you can't. Make the most of it."

"Are you sure?"

"I'm sure."

Lottie hesitated, but then she reached out and took the bundle, her fingers brushing against his. She looked at him and saw his blue eyes twinkling. It was such kindness that made her want to cry, and Lottie just about managed to stop that. She was able to smile in return and sat back.

"Thank you, Henry. That's very kind of you."

"Take care of yourself, Lottie." He pushed off the cart and winked at her. "Maybe we'll bump into each other again and you can return the favour."

Lottie stared after him as he went inside, waving at Amy before he disappeared. Amy and Billy put the baskets in the cart, Amy giving Lottie a bemused look.

"What was that all about?"

"Henry just gave me some of his lunch to eat," Lottie said timidly.

"Hmm." Amy raised her eyebrows. "Did he now? Well, if you are hungry, eat it now before we get back. Otherwise, the food will be taken off you."

Lottie didn't need to be told twice. Opening the bundle and giving the other sandwich to Billy as he clambered onto the cart, she began to eat. And it was the most delicious food she had tasted in a long time.

CHAPTER 4

1868

"Do you think we're ever going to get out of here?" Billy asked, turning away from the window.

Lottie flinched and looked over her shoulder. There was no one there, but she kept her voice low.

"You need to keep your voice down, Billy," she whispered. "We don't want to be caught in here when we're meant to be doing our chores."

"Sorry."

Billy jumped down from the bench and sat on the floor beside her. He brushed his hair out of his face, and Lottie wondered when he was going to get his hair cut again. The orphanage was meant to be strict on the boys having short hair, but they seemed to be neglecting those rules now.

"I hope we leave soon," Billy said, slumping against the side of the bookcase. "I hate it here. Sure, there are some nice people, and we have a roof over our heads, but I can't wait to leave."

"Same here." Lottie picked at the loose hem on her skirt. It was falling apart and needed sewing back together again. "I can't believe we've been here this long, and we're still here. Do people forget about children once they're put in these places?"

"They've forgotten about us." Billy paused. "Do you think Aunt Emily forgot about us?"

Lottie snorted.

"Of course she has. She didn't care about us in the first place. I don't even know why she carried on as long as she did when all she wanted to do was get rid of us as soon as possible."

"Maybe it was because she loved her sister and made a promise?"

"If she made a promise to look after us, she would've brought us into her home no matter what her husband said. But she didn't." Lottie scowled. "I think she was hoping we would die, and she wouldn't have to deal with us, but that didn't work."

Billy bit his lip.

"She doesn't hate us that much, does she?"

"What do you think, Billy? She was willing to let you die, after all."

Lottie didn't want to talk about Aunt Emily. She was a nasty woman who had abandoned them when they desperately needed her. She couldn't think about her without getting angry. Because of that woman, she could have lost her brother, and then she really would have been alone.

She wished this was not happening. She wanted to be back home with her parents, alive and well. But that wasn't going to be occurring anytime soon. Unless they somehow managed to get adopted out into a nice family, but Lottie doubted that was going to happen.

She was thirteen now, Billy eleven. They were too old to be considered cute for a prospective family looking to adopt, but not quite old enough to work in certain jobs that wouldn't end up killing them.

For now, they were stuck here. It was not something she was

comfortable with, but they had to make the most of it. And they had to keep their wits about them.

"How long are we going to stay here?" Billy whispered, looking around them.

"Do you mean in the library or in general?"

"Both? Either? I don't know."

Lottie sighed and put an arm around his shoulders.

"We'll stay here a bit longer. If we're lucky, nobody will notice we're gone at all."

She hoped that was the case. She was meant to be in the workshop with Mr Fletcher watching over them, and he always hovered a bit too close to Lottie. He made her skin crawl, especially with the way he looked at her. He kept following her around when he shouldn't, attempting to make conversation. Lottie did her best to escape him, part of the reason why she was hiding in the library.

If Mr Fletcher had sent someone to look for her, they would find her soon and she would get punished. Lottie wasn't looking forward to that, but she would rather suffer a punishment than be in that man's presence.

Why he was working there was beyond her, although Lottie had a feeling there was an ulterior motive to it all.

"Is there any of that cake left?" Billy asked, crossing his legs as he sat up.

Lottie rolled her eyes with a smile.

"You've eaten it all, Billy. There's none left. Henry only gave us a small bit."

"It was nice. I wanted some more."

"So do I, but there's only so much Henry can give us without anyone getting into trouble."

Billy pouted, which made Lottie fight back a laugh. Henry had been very kind to them since they met, often smuggling them food and other items. Lottie couldn't begin to count the number of books she had smuggled into a hiding place in the wall because of him. Somehow, she had managed to hide them without anyone noticing. If anyone was aware, they hadn't said anything.

Henry would also often come up to the orphanage and scale the wall during the night. Lottie would sneak out and they would sit in the far corner, behind the sheds, just talking. When Billy realised what they were doing, he insisted on joining them as well. It was nice to have something different, a fresh face who was nice to her without wanting anything in return.

Lottie was glad she had managed to make a friend. Henry seemed like one of the more loyal people she would come across. That was rare nowadays.

"Lottie! Where are you?"

Billy stiffened, his face paling.

"That's Amy!" he whispered frantically.

Silencing him with a finger to her lips, Lottie looked around the bookcase. She couldn't see Amy, but she could hear some footsteps. The librarian would be at her desk. She never left it, as far as Lottie knew, so she wouldn't be patrolling the aisles looking to make sure there were no wayward children. It was like she didn't care.

But Amy was sharper than that.

"What on earth are you two doing?"

Lottie jumped, and Billy let out a gasp before clamping his hands over his mouth. Amy was standing behind him, her arms folded as she watched them with a frown. She must have snuck along an aisle to creep up on them like that. Lottie scrambled to her feet, tugging Billy with her.

"We...I..."

"Are you trying to get out of work again?"

"No, of course not!" Lottie gulped. "It's just...well..."

"We haven't got time to discuss that," Amy cut her off. "You two need to come with me."

"Are we in trouble?" Billy whimpered, clutching onto his sister's hand. "We weren't being naughty."

But Lottie noticed something about Amy. The normally affable woman was troubled, something flickering behind her eyes. She looked uncomfortable. Lottie stepped towards her.

"What is it, Amy?"

"You need to get out of here."

"What?" Lottie blinked. "What do you mean? Out of the library?"

"No, out of the orphanage."

That took her by surprise. What did she mean by that? Lottie glanced at Billy, who looked equally confused.

"What do you mean by that? I can't exactly just walk out of here."

"This time, you might have to." Amy swallowed. "I don't say this to children, and the last time I said nothing I felt awful. I can't have it happen again."

"What's going on?"

"Not here." Amy beckoned them to follow her. "You need to come with me. Quickly, and be as quiet as you can."

Lottie had no idea what was going on, but what had happened was enough to make Amy spooked. Billy seemed to have the same idea as her as he trotted alongside her, both following Amy out of the library and into the hallway. Despite being as quiet as they could, it felt like their footsteps were echoing around them, making Lottie's ears ring.

They reached the landing above the main hall, where Amy urged them to slow down and keep out of sight. She paused at the corner, looking like she was committing espionage peeking around it. Then she crouched and crawled along, using the banister to keep mostly out of sight. She turned back and placed a finger to her lips before urging them to follow.

As she and Billy crawled after her to join the woman, Lottie heard voices in the main hall. And a familiar one made her heart stop. They were directly below them, so all Lottie could see was the top of Mr Fletcher's head, not the person he was talking to.

"I promise you, Mr Langley, this girl will be perfect for you. I've kept an eye on her over the years, and she's really blossoming."

"And you're sure that she'll be just what I'm looking for, Fletcher?" This voice was deeper, more gravely. "I don't want to have my time wasted."

"Oh, she's ideal. I think she's going to be a good worker." Mr Fletcher chuckled. "She's going to demand that her brother comes along as well. She won't go anywhere without him."

"Well, you're going to have to lie to her to make her come along. I'm not looking to have any boys around."

"I'll do what I can with that. Shall we go through to the sitting room? I'll have her sent for."

The voices faded away. Lottie stared at Amy.

"What's going on?" she whispered.

Amy sat up. She looked haggard.

"That's Mr Edward Langley. He's the owner of a mill further up the river in Buckinghamshire."

"That's a good thing, isn't it?" Billy asked. "Lottie gets to leave and work at a place that isn't here?"

"I wouldn't go without you, anyway," Lottie pointed out. "Not without you."

Amy shook her head.

"That's not his main business. It's just a cover. He...well, he procures women."

It took a moment for Lottie to realise what she was saying. Her mouth dropped open.

"He's...I know about those women in the streets. They have someone who oversees them, takes most of their money and makes sure they're looked after, for want of a better word. Are you talking about...?"

"Yes, I am," Amy answered, her expression grim. "Fletcher is one of those people who looks out for potentials in the orphanage. I don't know how they know each other, and I don't really want to. But he looks for…girls for Mr Langley, and then he gets paid for it."

* * *

Lottie couldn't believe what she was hearing. She was going to be sold off to someone? How was that even allowed? Wouldn't the warden of the orphanage stop it?

"But…can't we do something?" she asked desperately. "Shouldn't we tell the warden…?"

"I've tried to do that before, but I've been told that I'm misconstruing everything and I shouldn't listen to my overactive imagination," Amy said bitterly. "That was after the last time. I can't stand by and let this continue. The children here are innocent, and we we're meant to be looking after them, not selling them off for a few extra pennies."

"But how do we get out of here?" Billy looked fearful. "We can't just run away, can we? Where will we go?"

"We're going to have to do it right now," Amy replied. "Mr Fletcher is going to come looking for you, and you won't have a hope once he's gotten hold of you. Mr Langley is very strict and it's difficult for girls to leave. They're beaten into submission."

Lottie didn't want to talk about it any further. It scared her that this was happening at all. She wanted to curl into a ball and cry, to scream at the unfairness of it. What was wrong with people?

She wondered if she had enough time to go back and grab her books. If she could do that…

"We don't have time to get anything," Amy said, cutting through her thoughts. "Fletcher wouldn't let you take any of your things with you, anyway. You need to get out of here."

"But won't you get into trouble?" Lottie asked. "You're helping us run away."

Amy's expression was grim as she stood up and dusted herself down.

"I hate exploitation of children. It's cruel and ungodly. If I get into trouble, so be it." She grabbed Lottie's hand and pulled her to her feet. "Now come along. You've got to go now."

"Where will we go?" Billy clasped Lottie's other hand and got pulled along. "What do we do once we're gone?"

"Whatever you can, but as long as you don't get caught."

That was all Amy said as she hurried them down the stairs and managed to get them out of the front door. They were running towards the front gate, which was still open, when there was shouting coming from the house. Lottie began to panic. Did they mean they had been caught?

"Quick! Go!" Amy pushed them towards the gate. "You need to leave!"

"What about you?" Lottie grabbed at her. "Why don't you come with us?"

"You need a distraction. You're not going to get one if I go with you." Amy kissed their heads and gave them a quick hug each. "I'll be fine. I can take care of myself. Now go!"

Then Lottie saw Mr Fletcher appear in the doorway. He looked furious, his eyes widening when he saw them. Then he was hurrying towards them.

"Get back here!" he bellowed. "You're not going anywhere! Close the gates!"

The porter on the gates began to close them, and Lottie panicked even more. This was not how it was meant to go. She couldn't stay here.

Then Billy was pushing her towards the gates.

"Go!" he hissed. "Run!"

"What?"

"I'll distract him."

Lottie gawked at him, but Billy shook his head.

"It's not me he's after. You need to run."

"But I won't leave you!"

Billy's eyes were filled with tears as he hugged her tightly, pushing back before Lottie could fully grab onto him.

"You've protected me all these years, Lottie," he said, his voice thick. "Now let me protect my sister."

Then he turned and charged towards Mr Fletcher, catching him in the stomach with his head. Mr Fletcher groaned and collapsed to the ground, Billy throwing his arms and hitting him with loud bellows. Lottie stood there, stunned that she was witnessing this.

"Lottie, go!" Amy urged, pushing her towards the gates. "I'll look after Billy, but you need to leave!"

The gates were almost closed. If they shut, her options would diminish. Giving her brother one last look, she managed to get through the gap before the gates shut with a resounding clang behind her. She fell to the ground and lay there dazed, wondering what had just happened. She could hear shouting and Billy screaming angrily on the other side, and it made Lottie want to go back in. But she couldn't, not when she knew what lay in wait for her.

She had to run, and hope that Billy was left alone.

Which she did, her vision blinded by tears, and she stumbled down the street and into an alley.

CHAPTER 5

She had no idea where she was as she stumbled through the alleys. Lottie had been off the streets for some time now, and she couldn't get her bearings. She wanted to stop, but she didn't want to get caught. She needed to put distance between her and the orphanage.

She couldn't go back, even though it meant not knowing her brother was all right.

It was starting to get dark by the time Lottie slowed. She came to terraced houses that looked like they had been crammed together to get as many homes as possible into one place. They would have a coal house or something for her to hide in for a while. It would be dusty, but at least it would be dry; it was starting to rain, and Lottie didn't have a coat.

She went around the back of the houses and into the little yard they all shared. Ducking into the nearest coal bunker, she pushed herself into the corner as far as she could, trying to keep out of sight. It was so dusty that it made her cough, but at least it was warmer. Lottie wasn't sure how that worked. Maybe it was because it blocked the wind that had been picking up recently.

Curling herself into a ball, Lottie buried her face against her knees and let the tears take over. She sobbed, thinking about her brother and what might have happened. Would they have punished him badly? And what about Amy? She would be in trouble for what she did as well. And it was because of her.

No, not her. It was Mr Fletcher. He had planned to sell her to someone else, and he didn't care about it. It made her angry that this had happened because of him.

Most of all, Lottie blamed her aunt. Aunt Emily had discarded her and Billy because she didn't want to deal with either of them anymore. She had forced them into the orphanage, and Mr Fletcher had caught sight of her. If she had taken care of them, then none of this would be happening.

Lottie felt an intense hatred for her aunt then. That wasn't how family behaved.

She heard a gasp, and she looked up to see someone peering into the coal bunker, staring at her with wide eyes. Lottie pressed back against the wall, wishing she could disappear and pretend she hadn't been there.

"Oh, goodness, child! I thought I saw someone sneaking in here and thought someone was trying to steal my coal." The woman peered at her. "What on earth's going on?"

Lottie couldn't speak. She didn't know what to say. Then the woman grunted and lowered the poker she had been holding.

"Well, you can't stay out here. Not when it's going to rain. It's rather chilly at this time of year." She straightened up. "Come on, dear."

Lottie was in shock. Was she being shown some kindness? It felt strange to have that from someone who wasn't Amy or Henry. The woman sighed and held out a hand.

"Come along. You can't stay here. You'll feel better once you've gotten warm."

There was a little more hesitation, but then Lottie reached out and took her hand. It was warm and firm, and strong as she was pulled out of the bunker. The rain had

LOTTIE - THE RUNAWAY

picked up, and Lottie heard thunder overheard. It was going to turn into a huge downpour shortly. The woman tucked her into her side and hurried to the nearest house. They entered the kitchen, and the warmth practically hit Lottie in the face.

"I'm Mrs Alexandra Moore," the woman said, ushering her over to the table. "What's your name, dear?"

"Lottie," Lottie whispered. "Lottie Watson."

"Where did you come from?" Mrs Moore peered at her. "Did you run away from your family?"

That was enough to break the dam open, and Lottie started to cry harder. Without batting an eyelid, Mrs Moore steered her towards the fire, which was burning away strongly in the heather by the stove.

"Sit down here, dear," she said. "I'll be right back. And then you are going to tell me what's going on."

Lottie didn't know if she could tell her anything. Especially after what happened. She kept thinking about Amy and Billy, hoping they were going to be all right. She was sure Mr Fletcher was going to get into trouble, and he would take out his anger on them. If only she had struck him before she left.

After leaving the room for a moment, Mrs Moore returned with a blanket and put it around Lottie's shoulders. Then she made a hot chocolate, the smell of the chocolate wafting past Lottie's nose. Her stomach growled.

"Have you eaten, dear?"

"This morning," Lottie mumbled. "I missed lunch."

"No wonder you look so thin. I'm surprised you haven't snapped in half." Mrs Moore put the steaming cup into Lottie's hands before sitting in a comfortable-looking chair across from her. "Be careful, that drink is hot. Now talk to me. What's happened?"

Lottie had no idea why she was divulging everything to this stranger, but there was something soft and kindly about Mrs

Moore. She found herself telling the woman about what happened and where she had been.

She was crying throughout it all, but Mrs Moore was gentle with her, urging her to drink and get her strength back. She showed no judgement in her expression, but Lottie was sure she saw a tear in the woman's eye.

"That's so awful," Mrs Moore said when Lottie finished. She got out a handkerchief and dabbed at her eyes. "I can't believe anyone would treat children like that. You and your brother have been through so much."

"He was supposed to come with me," Lottie whispered. "And he told me to run. He didn't come with me."

"He was protecting you. That's what good siblings do. They look out for each other."

Lottie didn't know if that made her feel better. She sipped her hot chocolate. It was the tastiest thing she'd had that wasn't the cake Henry gave her.

"I don't know what to do now. Aunt Emily isn't going to take me in, and I can't go back. I need to find a way to find a job and get myself sorted. I refuse to go back to the orphanage, and I will not go anywhere near the workhouse."

"Given what you've said, I don't think going to the orphanage again is a good idea. And I agree with the workhouse." Mrs Moore frowned. "Why don't you stay here for now?"

"What?"

"It's just me here. My husband died three years ago, and I've got plenty of room for another person." She paused. "Well, I've only got one bed, but I keep the fire on all night, and the settee is comfortable. That should be something for now while we sort everything out."

Lottie didn't know what to say. This felt like a strange dream that she didn't want to wake up from. How was it possible that she had ended up meeting this kind woman?

"I...I don't want to take advantage..." she began.

"Nonsense! I'm not cold-hearted enough to send you back into the rain." Mrs Moore stood up. "I was about to make dinner. There will be plenty for both of us. And you look like you need a bit more meat on your bones."

Lottie wanted to cry again, this time at the kindness that a stranger was giving her. It was not something she anticipated. She managed a smile without breaking down.

"Thank you," she whispered.

* * *

IT TOOK a moment for Lottie to realise where she was when she opened her eyes. She stared at the ceiling, trying to figure out what was happening.

Then she remembered. She wasn't at the orphanage anymore. She was on a widow's settee with a fire burning away nearby. And it had been the most comfortable night's sleep she had ever had.

Lottie didn't want to get up, but she could hear Mrs Moore moving around the kitchen. Then she heard her voice.

"I felt my heart break seeing that poor thing in my coal bunker. She looked like she had been put through the wringer."

"And what you're saying about her treatment really happened?"

The second voice registered with Lottie, and she was sure she had heard it before. Sitting up, she listened.

"Yes, you could tell by the look in her eyes. That poor thing. I can't let her go back to that."

"You don't have to. I'm sure things can be figured out."

That voice. Lottie knew it. She couldn't believe it. Scrambling off the settee, she hurried into the kitchen. Mrs Moore was at the stove and Henry was sitting at the table. He stood up and stared at her when he saw her.

"Lottie?"

"Henry!"

She couldn't help herself, practically throwing herself at her friend. Henry caught her before they ended up on the floor and hugged her back. It made Lottie want to cry again. Then she pulled back and stared at him.

"What are you doing here?"

"Mrs Moore is my employer's sister." Henry nodded at the widow. "She also likes to spoil me with food, so I come over every morning."

"A growing child needs what he can get," Mrs Moore said fondly. She gave Henry a bemused look. "I didn't realise you knew Lottie."

"She comes to deliver the paper at the printers. We've talked a few times." Henry's eyes searched Lottie's face. "What are you doing here? Where's Billy?"

"Let's not discuss that right now," Mrs Moore said quickly as Lottie's throat tightened. "Both of you need some food in your bellies, and then we need to figure out what we do going forward. Especially for little Miss Lottie here."

Lottie saw Henry's expression change to one of more confusion, but she was glad of the interlude. She didn't want to go through what happened the day before; it would just have her crying again, and it had exhausted her before. She needed a moment to get used to the fact Henry was here before her.

Mrs Moore placed a plate piled with food in front of both children, and Lottie's stomach growled loudly at the sight. She hadn't seen so much nice food in one sitting. Mrs Moore smiled.

"I'll take that as a compliment if you're that hungry," she said. "Eat up."

Lottie didn't need to be told twice. Like the food the widow had cooked the day before, it was delicious, and soon she was wiping her plate with a hunk of bread. Henry was doing the same, almost matching her for each mouthful. There was no talking until they were done and both children were slumping back in their chairs.

Mrs Moore laughed and cleared the plates away.

"Now that is one way to make a lady feel good about herself. When everyone eats her food."

"It was delicious, Mrs Moore," Lottie said fervently. "It's been a long time since I've had a good meal."

"I've had plenty of time to practise. My husband and I lived comfortably enough, but not enough to hire servants, so I learned to do everything myself." Mrs Moore came back to the table and sat down, patting her hands on the table. "Right, to business."

Lottie glanced at Henry, who shrugged.

"She's just a very practical woman, that's all."

"A practical woman who needs to decide what I'm going to do with the girl I found running away," Mrs Moore said sharply. "The poor thing can't go back there, and I wouldn't be comfortable letting authorities know."

Lottie shook her head.

"I can't. Not when…" She didn't think she could say it in front of Henry, but she tried. "When I was going to be sold off."

Henry's eyes widened. Then they narrowed and he scowled.

"Those…I'll…"

"Henry, calm down," Mrs Moore said gently. "That's not going to get us anywhere. For now, I think getting Lottie settled is the priority."

"And getting Billy out," Lottie said quickly.

"What happened to Billy?" Henry asked. "I thought he would be with you."

Before Lottie could form her words, Mrs Moore was talking, sounding like the strict headteacher Lottie used to have when she was a little girl.

"It's just me living here alone, and if we manage to get another cot and mattress, we can set it up in the corner of the room. Or we can clear out the room at the back…" She faltered. "My husband's office, you see. Even though it's been some years since his death…"

She didn't finish the sentence, but Lottie didn't need her to. She understood that grief could affect people in different ways, and sometimes it meant not touching something of theirs in the hopes it would remain the same once the person came back. It was a far-fetched thing to believe, but when someone loved another so fiercely it was hard to let them go.

"So we can clear out the back room and Lottie could sleep in there," Henry suggested. "I can ask a few people for help, if you need it."

"Thank you, Henry." Mrs Moore's voice was thick as she patted his hand. "You're a good boy."

"And what about a job?" Henry nodded at Lottie. "I know Lottie's not someone who slacks. She likes to work hard, and I know she'll put her mind to whatever she can."

"Yes!" Lottie nodded vigorously. "I will. Anything to make myself useful."

Mrs Moore peered at her. In her state, Lottie hadn't paid much attention to her the previous day. She was probably in her forties, her dark hair streaked with white and lines on the corners of her eyes and mouth. Her hazel eyes had a slight twinkle to them, and she carried her hourglass figure with her head held high. She had a confidence to her that Lottie wished that she had. It would be nice to be able to walk around and not worry about everyone around her.

"What sort of jobs are you prepared to do?" Mrs Moore asked.

"Anything," Lottie said a little too quickly, before adding, "Within reason, of course. I know I have limitations, but I'll take what I can."

The widow tilted her head to one side and regarded her thoughtfully. It made Lottie want to squirm in her chair, but she stopped herself.

"Well, how about you work for me as a maid?" the woman

suggested. "I won't be able to pay much, but it will be a good starting point. You can learn how to work in service with me, and it will give you the experience that you need. Plus, you'll have room and board here, and I won't charge rent."

Lottie sat up.

"Really? I can work for you?"

"How old are you, dear?"

"I'm thirteen. Nearly fourteen."

"I see." Mrs Moore nodded. "Well, you're going to be starting a bit late, but if you're a quick learner it shouldn't be a problem. We can do that in the mornings, and then in the afternoons you and I will go over your lessons and what you need to catch up on."

Lottie's mouth fell open.

"I'll get lessons as well?"

"You don't want to rely on other people to read, write, and do sums for you, do you?"

"No, of course not." Lottie gulped. "My studies stopped shortly after I turned thirteen. And I've been reading a lot when I'm not doing my chores."

"That's good. We can work on that. It will help you with extra things in your life. It also makes you more desirable when it comes to getting jobs because you can read and write." Mrs Moore looked pleased. "Sounds like you're a bright young girl, dear. Helping you out shouldn't be a problem."

Lottie wondered if she was still asleep. Henry chuckled and gently kicked her under the table.

"You're not dreaming, Lottie. This is really happening."

"I...I still don't believe it."

"Believe it, dear." Mrs Moore laid a hand over hers. "I'm not a monster, and I'm certainly not going to let you be taken back by those people. You're safe here, and you can be confident with that."

Lottie believed that. She really did.

CHAPTER 6

*1*873

"That's all of my work done, Mrs Leonard," Lottie said, placing her basket on the table. "I've got it all done."

"You're very quick, Lottie." Mrs Leonard looked at her over the top of her spectacles. "You've checked and double-checked your work, have you?"

"Yes, ma'am. It's all done to your specifications."

Lottie waited nervously as her employer took each item out of the basket and inspected the work closely. She was always finishing before everyone else, people who had worked longer than her at the dressmakers, and it made her a little embarrassed that it appeared she was rushing. But her work was always good, so she knew she should relax a little.

After a while, Mrs Leonard nodded her approval.

"I'm impressed. I've not had anyone work as fast as you and have good final articles to prove it. It's good."

"Thank you, Mrs Leonard."

Her employer began to fold the items and put them back into the basket, giving Lottie a smile.

"If you're done, you can head home. But you must remember

to be here bright and early. We've got those dress fittings, and I want you to be present to help."

"Of course."

Collecting her things, Lottie left the shop and took a deep breath of warm, summer air, a gentle breeze wafting around her. It was comforting to know that her new job was going well. She had only been at the shop for two weeks after a recommendation from her previous employer, and it was good.

The pay was better than she thought, which would make Mrs Moore happy. She hadn't raised the rent at all since Lottie turned eighteen four months ago, but she would be pleased her charge was improving day by day.

Lottie wondered if she should buy something for her landlady as a way of saying thank you. The other jobs she had taken on were good and came with a good word from Mrs Moore, and Lottie had not disappointed. The widow's teachings had worked, and the ability to pick up and carry on as if she had been doing the job all her life was remarkable. Lottie couldn't believe that she was now in such demand. It was strange.

But in a good way. Lottie was looking forward to furthering herself as a seamstress. It was her favourite job for now.

"Lottie!"

Lottie looked around and her heart skipped when she saw Henry walking towards her, his hat slightly lopsided on his head. He looked rather flushed, slowing a little as he reached her.

"Henry, what are you doing here?" Lottie looked at the church clock across the street. "I thought you were going to be in the office still."

"I would've been, but I said I had an emergency so I could leave." Henry grinned at her. "I wanted to walk you home."

Lottie couldn't help but laugh.

"You didn't need to call it an emergency, though. You're going to get into trouble if your employer finds out what you did."

Henry shrugged.

"It's worth it. Anyway, are you heading back to Mrs Moore's?"

"In a moment, I wanted to get something for her."

"Like what?"

Henry offered his arm, and Lottie slipped her arm through his as they walked down the street. It was something they had done many times before, even with Lottie's previous jobs. Henry would meet her whenever he was able to, and they went for a walk. Sometimes, they would have tea in a restaurant before walking through the park and heading back to Mrs Moore's house.

With Henry's new job working in the newspaper as one of the writers, they had a bit more money for frivolities. Lottie had said a few times she was uncomfortable about Henry spending so much money on her, but he claimed he didn't mind. It was something he would do happily for her.

Lottie felt warm and happy knowing that he was looking after her. She liked it. Henry was a dear friend, and he had been looking out for her in the last five years since she settled in with Mrs Moore.

"He's growing up into such a fine young man," Mrs Moore had declared not too long ago after Henry had escorted Lottie home. "And very handsome, too."

"Handsome?" Lottie had been confused at that. "I haven't noticed."

"Oh, you haven't?" Her landlady had given her a sly smile and winked at her. "Well, I know for a fact he's noticed how pretty you've become. He can't take his eyes off you."

"That's not true!" Lottie had protested before her cheeks got warm. "He doesn't!"

But that interaction had been on her mind since, and now Lottie couldn't stop herself from looking at Henry as they spent more time together. He was handsome. He was several inches taller, broad-shouldered, and well-built. His clothes were smart, cutting him into a fine figure. And his smile made Lottie's stomach flutter at the mere sight of it. It was just beautiful.

Now whenever he was around, she couldn't stop thinking about it. It made her wonder if she was seeing him differently or if it was due to Mrs Moore's attempt at a match. She had been subtly pushing them together over the years, and Lottie had caught the woman smiling in a corner when she and Henry were spending time together.

Did Henry see her as attractive? Lottie didn't know, but she was certainly too shy to ask.

They passed by a shop with a huge window, and Lottie caught sight of herself. She was still petite, barely coming up to Henry's shoulder, her hair pinned up under her hat and her frame willowy. She looked a bit like a waif, but Mrs Moore said it was a pretty appearance that made heads turn. Lottie didn't know about that. She was certainly striking, and it was hard to believe she was grown up now, but nothing about her would turn heads.

Not that she knew, anyway.

As they passed a confectioners' shop, Lottie turned to Henry.

"Why don't we get some sweets for her?" she suggested.

"Sweets?"

"Mrs Moore loves them. She's always sucking on a hard boiled sweet."

Henry chuckled.

"I'm surprised that woman has any teeth left after all those sweets. She's going to be toothless by the time she's sixty."

"At least she's happy," Lottie shot back with a smile. "Why not? Or we can get a cake from the bakery just down the street? Something to cheer the evening up."

Henry arched an eyebrow in amusement, but then he nodded with a smile that made Lottie a little lightheaded.

"All right. If it will make you happy. But I'll buy it for you."

"There's no need..."

"Nonsense, it'll be fine. You save for everything else." Henry squeezed her hand. "I know you've got your plans to look forward to. I'm just giving you a hand."

Lottie knew what he was talking about. Henry was referring to Billy. It had been five years and Lottie had no idea where Billy was. Mrs Moore had asked a couple of friends for help, and they went to the orphanage to look for Billy, but he was gone. The warden said Billy was taken to a factory to work, and they couldn't help. And refused to say where Billy had gone. Lottie was worried that Mr Langley had taken him, but that route was far-fetched. Amy was gone as well, having been fired for her behaviour during Lottie's escape. Nobody knew, or cared, where she had gone, either.

Lottie felt awful that she hadn't been able to protect her brother. He had done a selfless act to help her get away, and she hadn't been able to return the favour. Now he was gone, and she had no idea where he was. Not a word for five years, and the pain of not knowing was agonising. Lottie tried her best to ignore it, but that was easier said than done. She missed him dreadfully, hoping that he was all right and safe.

She wasn't about to stop because she didn't know where he was. But knowing where to start again was easier said than done.

"Here we go." Henry's voice drew Lottie out of her trance as they approached the bakery. "Which one would you like? I know she likes both chocolate and the Victoria sponge. Which one do you think we should get?"

"Either one is fine." Lottie looked at the assortment on display. The sight of them was making her mouth water. "Just be quick, otherwise I'm going to end up wanting more than just one cake."

Henry chuckled and tapped her nose affectionately.

"Then I'll be as slow as possible."

"Henry!"

Still laughing, he entered the bakery and got into line. As he started talking to the assistant, Lottie looked at the cakes and marvelled at how things were intricately made. She wondered if she could get a chance to work in a bakery. It looked incredible to bake cakes and bread. But the work hours were terrible, sometimes having to stay up all night or something close to it to make sure the bread was ready. Lottie didn't think she could cope with it.

"Like what you see, do you?"

Lottie gasped and spun around. A tall, slim man with bright red hair and a trimmed red beard was standing behind her, leaning on his cane and giving her a lazy smile. His green eyes fixed on her, and Lottie could barely pull herself away from them. They had her rooted to the spot.

And she couldn't believe how quickly her heart pounded when she saw how handsome he was. Especially when he smiled. It made her weak at the knees.

What was happening to her?

"I...sorry?"

Why did she have to squeak like that? It wasn't how she normally spoke. Clearing her throat, Lottie tried to not sound like a simpleton. The gentleman's smile widened.

"You like cakes, do you? Wondering which one you're going to have?"

"Yes. No!" Lottie coughed, wishing she wasn't stumbling over her own words. "Actually, my friend and I have figured out what we wanted. He's just inside buying one."

"Oh, you and your friend, is it?"

There was something vaguely familiar about him, and for a moment, Lottie couldn't put her finger on it. He gave her a slight bow.

"Forgive me, I was rude not to introduce myself. Oscar Preston."

"Lottie Watson."

Oscar's eyes flashed as he looked at her.

"Lottie. That's a pretty name." He tilted his head to one side.

"I've not seen you around here. Are you new to the area? I think I would have noticed someone as attractive as you walking around."

Was he flirting with her? It did feel like he was flattering her quite a bit. Lottie was momentarily speechless. She had no idea what to say in response. She simply stared at him. This made her look even more stupid in his eyes. How was she able to talk coherently when he was being so charismatic with her?

Lottie wasn't used to it.

Licking her dry lips, she tried.

"I...I've been in the area for a while," she mumbled. "I don't live too far away."

"Oh, really?" He raised his eyebrows. "Whereabouts?"

"Not far."

Lottie wasn't about to tell him where she lived. Mrs Moore said that she shouldn't tell just anyone her address. Ladies had to be careful who they trusted with things, including their homes. Although she had a feeling Mrs Moore wouldn't mind if she saw the handsome man before her.

Why wasn't her heart slowing down and going at a pace that didn't make her dizzy?

"And you're walking around here without a chaperone?" Oscar tittered. "You know, someone could come along and take advantage of you."

"I'm not alone," Lottie protested. "My friend's inside. He'll be out any moment."

"Oh, will he?"

His mouth twitched, and Lottie wished that she would stop staring. It was beginning to make her squirm. She didn't like the attention on her, but at the same time she didn't want it to stop.

"So, Mr...Preston...what is it that you do? Do you work around here?"

"Oh, me? I just work in Whitehall, that's all." Oscar shrugged as if it wasn't a big issue for him. "And I also have a couple of businesses that are quite successful. Let's just say my days are very busy."

"And yet you're standing here talking to me?" Lottie shot back.

Oscar threw back his head and laughed. It was a deep laugh that made Lottie feel like she had warm shivers going up her spine. What had just happened there?

"I'm having a rare evening going for a walk and not doing anything else. I was meant to be enjoying my own company, so you can imagine my surprise when I see a beautiful young lady on her own." He winked. "I just had to make her acquaintance."

Lottie put her hands on her hips.

"And do you normally speak in such a manner to these young ladies?"

"What manner?"

"Flirtatiously."

Oscar looked amused, leaning on his black cane. Lottie saw the silver head on the end. It looked like it cost double her rent. This man had a lot of money, and it was making her a little uncomfortable.

"When a woman deserves to be treated in such a manner, that's what I'll do." Oscar sounded as if it was obvious he would be flirtatious. "And you deserve to have compliments lavished on you."

"A bit strong, don't you think?"

At least her confidence was coming back. Oscar shrugged.

"At least women know my intentions. I like to be plain about it."

"What's going on, Lottie?"

Lottie jumped. She had momentarily forgotten about Henry. He was stepping out of the bakery with a cake box in his hands. He looked from Lottie to Oscar and narrowed his eyes. Oscar didn't look the slightest bit annoyed, merely smirking at him. Lottie gulped.

"I...this is Oscar Preston. Henry Lewis is my friend."

She noticed that way Henry glanced at her, almost as if he wasn't happy with the way she addressed him. He gave Oscar a brisk nod.

"Mr Preston."

"Mr Lewis." Oscar's response was cool and smooth. Then his gaze was back on Lottie. "I hope we'll bump into each other again, Lottie. I'd be honoured to make your acquaintance further."

Touching his fingers to his head, he turned and sauntered away, tapping his cane on the cobbles as he went. Lottie watched him go, admiring the way he walked and his confident stride. There was something about him that was very impressive, and she couldn't look away.

"What on earth did he want?" Henry asked grumpily.

"Oh!" Lottie turned. "He just wanted to say hello and introduce himself."

Henry scowled.

"It was clear what he wanted from you."

Lottie gasped.

"Henry! There's no need to speak like that! He was being a perfect gentleman."

"But I saw the way he looked at you. That man does not have a pure thought in his head, especially when it comes to ladies."

Lottie stared at him. She hadn't heard Henry speak like this before, and now he looked close to angry that Oscar had even paid her any attention.

"What is wrong with you?" she demanded.

"If you don't know what his intentions were, then you're naiver than you make yourself out to be, Lottie." Henry shook his head. "He has his eyes on a certain prize, and not for good reasons."

"Stop it!" Lottie held up a hand. "You're starting to sound

ridiculous. Can't a gentleman talk to a young woman without people thinking scandalously?"

"Normally, I would, but I know men like him. I've encountered them plenty of times in my job."

"Well, don't put all of the men in the same boat," Lottie said coolly. She held out a hand. "Give me the cake."

"Lottie…"

"I'll walk home on my own. I think it's best that you head home yourself."

Henry looked surprised. He didn't hand over the cake.

"Don't be silly, Lottie. You can't say we're separating now because I was making an observation."

"I can. It's not far, and I don't appreciate you treating me like I don't know what I'm doing. I was simply making conversation, and he was nice to me, that's it." Lottie glared at him. "If you can refrain from making remarks about someone you know nothing about, you can walk me back to the house. But if you can't, give me the cake and leave."

Henry sighed heavily and his shoulders slumped.

"All right, fine. I'll say nothing about Mr Preston. Are you satisfied?"

She wasn't, but Lottie would take it. She didn't like this side of Henry. It was almost as if he was jealous.

That threw her a little. What did Henry have to be jealous about? They weren't courting. They were merely friends.

Now Lottie really didn't know what to think. Everything was twirling around in her head, and she couldn't get it to stop.

CHAPTER 7

"It's beautiful, isn't it?"

Lottie jumped. She could see Oscar in the reflection of the window. She was standing at the jewellery shop, looking at the various gorgeous items on display. Her heart thumping, Lottie turned and smiled at him.

"Good day, Mr Preston."

"Call me Oscar, please." He raised his hat to her. "Mr Preston makes me feel so old."

"But isn't that rather informal?"

"Well, I'm the only one who is going to complain, and if I don't..."

Lottie couldn't help but smile. She couldn't deny that she was pleased to see Oscar again. It had been a week since their paths crossed, and he kept popping in and out of her thoughts. She didn't know why, but it made her smile thinking about him. Even with their brief interaction, it played again in her mind.

Was it because he was handsome and paying her attention? Was it due to being older than her? Lottie wasn't sure, but she had a feeling Oscar was somewhere in his mid to late twenties.

LOTTIE - THE RUNAWAY

Or was it something else? Whatever it was, Lottie knew she was drawn to him.

Now they were looking at each other, and she was excited about it. He was dressed in a smart dark suit that had no creases in sight. Everything about him was immaculate, and the confidence excluded from him.

"I didn't think I was going to run into you here," she said, wondering if she could say something that didn't make her sound so stupid. Couldn't she think of a better sentence?

"I was on a walk after lunch, and I just happened to see you by chance. It feels like the stars are aligned for me."

Lottie couldn't help but snort at that.

"You don't believe in all of that, do you?"

"Depends on the time of day." Oscar's smile was making Lottie lightheaded. "You're on your own, are you? No guard dog standing by you?"

"Guard dog?"

"That young man you were with last time I saw you."

Lottie frowned.

"Henry isn't a guard dog. He's a very dear friend who's helped me out over the years."

"Oh, really?" Oscar sniggered, leaning on his cane. "From the way he behaved, I have a feeling he sees himself as more than a friend."

Lottie didn't know what to say to that. Henry saw her as that. It didn't make sense. He was someone who always told her what he was thinking. Why wouldn't he say that to her?

"You didn't know that he likes you?" Oscar asked.

"He's my friend," Lottie said faintly.

"Trust me, the way he glared at me suggested that he didn't like any other gentleman talking to you. He's rather territorial." Oscar looked her up and down. "I can't blame him, though. If I had a beautiful woman like you on my arm, I would certainly feel the same way."

Lottie's face felt warm, and she twisted her fingers together. What did she say to that? She was complimented on her looks many times before, but she often brushed it off. She wasn't interested in how beautiful she was when there were more practical things to do. But hearing it coming from Oscar was something else. It made her feel lighter, happier.

And she was left a little speechless.

"Would you like to walk with me?" Oscar asked. "I'm going for a walk around the park, and I wouldn't mind having a lovely companion with me."

"That…that's very kind of you…" Lottie held up her hands as he held an arm out. "But I've got to get back to work. I got distracted as I went past, but I'm going to be late if I don't get back to the shop."

"I see." His eyes twinkled as he lowered his arm. "You never stop, do you?"

"Not really. It's a busy time for us right now, and I don't want to get behind."

Why was she turning him down? Lottie knew she had plenty of time to get back to the shop, but she had a feeling she was going to be distracted even more if she was in Oscar's presence. There was something about him that drew her in, and it was refusing to let her go.

"Then perhaps another time?" he suggested. "Might I have the pleasure of escorting you?"

"You?" Lottie squeaked. "You want to escort me?"

"Of course. Why wouldn't I want to be more acquainted with a beautiful woman?"

"But…I'm not of your social class, am I?" Lottie stuttered. "I'm a seamstress, and you're…well, you're clearly superior to me."

"So what? I can be around whoever I want." Oscar reached into his pocket and pulled out a little notebook. Along with a gold-topped pen, he held it out to Lottie. "Why don't you write down your address for me, and I'll call on your next day off?"

Lottie hesitated. Mrs Moore had been very strict about this, and she had been sticking to that. She didn't want to get into trouble, even if Oscar did seem like a harmless individual. Making up her mind, she took the notebook and scribbled down the name of the nearest park to her home, along with when she was next off. He raised his eyebrows when he got it back.

"You don't live in a park, do you?"

"It's where I'll meet you." Lottie lifted her chin and straightened up. "Twelve-thirty at the park on Thursday. I'll see you then."

And with that, she turned and walked away, smiling to herself as she left Oscar. She was not going to make it look like she was a woman who would say yes so easily. She might have agreed to a meeting, but she wasn't going to give him everything.

She was sure she heard Oscar laughing as she walked away and turned a corner. The shop wasn't too far away, so she wouldn't be late. Not by much, anyway.

Lottie was almost at the shop when she bumped into someone in front of her. Hands grabbed at her arms as she wobbled.

"Slow down there! I thought you were going to knock me over."

"What?" Lottie looked up and blinked. "Henry! What are you doing here?"

"I was coming back from an assignment, and thought I'd come by to see how you were." Henry looked bemused. "What happened to you?"

"Me?"

"You're looking rather flushed. And there's a sparkle about you I haven't seen before."

Lottie didn't know about a sparkle. She had felt a little lighter talking to Oscar, but that was it. She wasn't about to tell Henry that, though; that would just result in her friend getting upset, and Lottie hated upsetting anyone.

"No reason," she said quickly. "It's just a nice day, and I'm in a good mood."

"Oh, really?" Henry didn't look convinced. "Right."

"Did you want something else, Henry? Much as I would love to talk, I've got to get back to work."

"Oh. Right." Slightly flushed, Henry rubbed the back of his neck. "I was wondering, after work, if you wanted to go and get something to eat? There's a new restaurant nearby that's opened and I wanted to take you there."

"Of course." Lottie didn't need to think about it. "I always love exploring new places with you, especially restaurants."

Henry looked relieved, which confused Lottie. They always spent time together after work. Most days, they would go and have something to eat, and other times they just went for walks. It was nothing different to what they usually did, but there was something about Henry's demeanour that shifted everything a little.

What was going on?

"Right. Yes." Henry seemed to shake himself out of his daze and cleared his throat. "Well, I'll be heading back to the office, then. I'll pick you up outside the shop at the usual time?"

"The usual time," Lottie agreed. She squeezed his hands, feeling his warm fingers clasp around hers. "I'll see you later."

"Right." Henry swallowed and his cheeks flushed. "Later."

Then he hurried away, crossing the street almost right in front of a horse and carriage. The driver shouted at him, and Henry ducked his head and practically ran to the other side of the street, bumping into a crossing sweeper at the same time. Lottie watched as he apologised to the young man before leaving as quickly as he could. It was rare to see him like this, and she wondered what was going on with him.

Mrs Leonard was at the counter when Lottie entered the shop. She gave her a knowing look over her spectacles.

"Looks like your gentleman friend was rather flustered," she remarked.

"Gentleman friend?" Lottie frowned. "Henry's a friend, nothing else to it."

"Are you sure? He's here every day to walk you home, sometimes to meet you for lunch, and he was hovering outside for a while as well." Mrs Leonard gave her a sly smile. "Looks like someone's quite sweet on you, Lottie."

That gave Lottie pause. She had never seen it like that. Well, the thought had crossed her mind before, but she had dismissed it. Henry was just looking out for her.

"I don't think he is," she mumbled. "He's known me for years. We're just close, that's all."

Mrs Leonard sighed and took off her spectacles, polishing them with her handkerchief.

"Dear, I've been married a long time, but I remember when I was near your age and met my husband. I saw him as a friend, nothing more. But as time went on, feelings changed, and I felt like everything just fell into place. It was one of those things that crept up on me when I was least expecting it. My guess is that's going to happen to you soon, if it hasn't already and you have no idea how you really feel about Mr Henry Lewis."

Lottie didn't know what to say to that. She had never had any kind of conversation with her employer about her friendship with Henry, only in passing with the other seamstresses. But she never thought anyone would get the impression that there was something more.

"I...well..."

"You don't have to think about it too much now. You've got work to do." Mrs Leonard put her spectacles back on. "But I think you two would make a sweet-looking couple. Mr Lewis is a nice young man, and I think you would be doing him an injustice if you turn him away." She held up her hands. "But that's my opinion. You do what you need to do. Anyway, are you going to get back to work? Your basket is still half-full, so you need to get on with it."

Lottie didn't know what to say. Mrs Leonard was trying to do something akin to matchmaking? She wasn't sure how to feel about that.

She went to her workstation in a daze. It couldn't be right, could it? Henry was just a friend. There was nothing romantic about it.

People were just seeing things that weren't there, weren't they?

* * *

"Is Henry coming over later, Lottie?" Mrs Moore asked as Lottie entered the sitting room.

"I don't believe so." Lottie looked at the clock on the mantlepiece. "He said that he had a lot of work to do lately, so he's been burning the candle at both ends."

Her landlady frowned.

"He's going to collapse and make himself ill if he carries on like this. I don't like that he's hurting himself in such a manner."

"He'll be fine, Mrs Moore." Lottie sat on the settee and opened her book. "Henry's tougher than you think. He'll come by and see us soon."

"Although I have a feeling he's not going to be impressed if he does come by and you're entertaining someone else," Mrs Moore grunted.

Lottie blinked in surprise. She hadn't heard that tone from the widow in a long time. It sounded as if she was unhappy with the situation in front of her.

"What do you mean by that?" she asked. "Is something wrong?"

Mrs Moore sighed and put aside her sewing, dusting down

her skirts. She still wore black and was always very put together. But she looked graceful and composed, something Lottie was a little envious about. She wished she could look as impressive as her landlady. Eccentric as she was, she knew how to take care of herself. If anything, Mrs Moore seemed to be looking younger as the days went by. She said it was because of Lottie's presence, which was flattering.

Lottie hoped she was like that when she was of a similar age.

"Well, I'm a little worried about you, Lottie."

"How so?"

"I understand that you're an attractive young lady, and there are going to be plenty of gentlemen wanting your attention. But I feel that you're going to get yourself into a lot of trouble being around two young men."

Lottie stared at her, wondering if she had heard her correctly.

"Are you saying I'm playing both men?"

"I'm not saying that at all. But you might get pulled in different directions, and it's going to be a difficult thing for you to handle when you finally have to choose." Mrs Moore pursed her lips. "I know this is making me sound biased towards Henry —and I am very fond of him—but I'm worried that people are going to get hurt, and whichever outcome it's going to be, you and Henry are going to become casualties."

Lottie was confused. Was Mrs Moore telling her that she was in danger of breaking hearts? She couldn't believe what was going on. She never thought she was capable of that.

"But…it's nothing serious," she protested. "I'm not even seeing either of them romantically."

"Are you sure about that?"

"What do you mean?"

Mrs Moore smoothed her hair back and settled into her chair.

"I was married for several years, and while I lost my husband years ago, I know about love and the heart. It's clear that you've had your fancy taken by Henry and this Mr Oscar Preston, and you're enjoying the attention from both."

Lottie gasped.

"Mrs Moore! I'm not that sort of person!"

"Are you not? Henry's been following you around for years. It's clear to me that he loves you." Mrs Moore sighed. "And Mr Preston…sure, he's a charming man and he has a lot of interest in you, but there is something about him that makes me nervous about your wellbeing."

"How so?"

"You barely know anything about him, for a start."

"I know things about him!" Lottie retorted, annoyance building in her chest. "We talk a lot. He's told me about himself!"

"You mean about how he's involved in a lot of businesses and that they're doing very well?" Mrs Moore shot back. "And that's the reason he walks around in nice clothes and talks about the expensive things he has?"

Lottie stared at her. As far as she was aware, when she had entertained Oscar at the house, Mrs Moore hadn't been in the room. She said she was giving them space to talk while being close by.

"Have you been eavesdropping? Mrs Moore, don't you trust me?"

"It's not you that I don't trust, Lottie." The widow didn't even blink at the accusation. "But Oscar Preston is something else. I don't know what it is, but he puts me on edge. Especially when you know practically nothing about him personally."

"But I…"

Lottie faltered when she realized that Mrs Moore was right. She had talked to Oscar about herself and what had happened during her childhood, something that he had found shocking. He even commented how he admired her for the way she had gotten through it all and grown stronger as a result. But now that she thought about it, she realised that he had never talked about himself. Not the way she did, anyway. Every time Lottie asked him a question about his childhood, his family, or anything that didn't involve money and his business, Oscar would give her a vague response before swiftly turning it back on her. At the time, Lottie had been flattered that he was focused on her and making her feel noticed. But now she was beginning to wonder why she knew nothing about him.

"Maybe he doesn't like talking about himself?" she suggested desperately. "Perhaps he's interested in knowing more about me?"

"That may be true, but if you don't know anything about him then something's not quite right. You should know just a little about him, otherwise the foundations are very shaky."

Lottie took a deep breath. She didn't like the annoyance building inside her, twisting into a knot in her chest. She had been seeing Oscar for the past month, and he had been incredibly charming. He had taken her to the theatre to see many plays, including a few operas. They had dined at fine restaurants, and he took her for walks around the park. It felt nice to be on his arm and to get envious looks from every lady as they walked past.

He had charmed her to the point that Lottie hung onto his every word, and yet she didn't know anything about him. How was that possible?

"I feel like you're trying to push me more towards Henry," she remarked. "You don't like Oscar, and you want me to be with Henry instead."

"It's nothing of the sort. However, if you're going to make a choice, you need to make an informed one." Mrs Moore gave her a firm stare. "Henry's never lied to you, has he?"

"Well..."

"And you know a lot about him, don't you? He's been open to you with everything from the start."

Lottie faltered. She knew that the other woman was right, but it still felt like she was being pushed towards Henry and turned away from Oscar. It didn't feel as if she was being given a chance to decide of her own.

She put her book aside and stood up.

"I think I might just get some fresh air outside," she murmured, dusting herself down. "I...I need to think."

"All right, dear. Take your time."

At least she wasn't being pushed any further. Lottie didn't need her head feeling more confused than she already was. Leaving the sitting room, she headed through the hall and out the front door. Wandering down the steps, she crossed the street and into the park through the small gate that was barely used, hearing it creak as she opened it. There were a few tree trunks sticking out of the ground from when the trees had been chopped down a few months before, turning into makeshift seats. It was where Lottie sat whenever she needed some quiet time alone. Just off the path and behind the bushes, it was secluded.

Nobody knew she was there. Lottie needed that right now.

She sagged onto one of the stumps and rubbed her hands over her face. Why was this turning into something complicated? Lottie hadn't considered her and Henry as courting each other. They were just friends who saw each other regularly and spent a lot of time together. But the longer it had gone on, Lottie found herself wondering if this was what it would be like having a husband.

She felt happy and relaxed whenever Henry was with her. He was comforting, a familiar person who made Lottie feel good about herself. Her spirits were always good around him.

Was he in love with her? Lottie didn't know. She was too scared to think about it. That might change things between them, and she didn't think she could cope with that if Henry started avoiding her.

Then there was Oscar. Her heart fluttered whenever he was near her, his smile making her weak at the knees. He gave her attention that Lottie enjoyed. It made her feel as if she was the only woman in the world. But hearing Mrs Moore remind her that she knew nothing about him brought things back to reality.

Two men were in her life, and both appeared to want her attention. Oscar tried to monopolise her time, but Lottie drew a line there. She wasn't going to neglect Henry for anything. She would not do that to him. And she could tell that Henry was relieved to have her time and attention. He wasn't happy about her being around Oscar, but he kept his remarks mostly to himself unless Lottie confronted him. She was glad about that, but at the same time, she wished that he would say something, and they could argue.

But that could have her avoiding him more, and Lottie didn't want to lose him. Henry had always been there for her, and she couldn't have that taken away.

And yet it felt uncomfortable splitting her time between the two of them.

She buried her head in her hands. What was going on? Why was she having this problem? Couldn't she just have a normal life?

Suddenly, the problems she had at the orphanage were nothing compared to deciding which man she should be giving more attention to.

"Lottie?"

Lottie jumped with a gasp. She looked up and saw Henry stepping around the bushes. He looked like he hadn't slept much lately with dark circles under his circles, his face pale. Lottie got to her feet.

"Henry? What are you doing here?"

"I thought I'd see how you were doing. Mrs Moore said you had gone for some air, so I thought I'd come here."

"But how...?"

Henry smiled.

"I know you, Lottie. I know where you like to go when you

need a moment to yourself." He approached and settled on the stump beside her. "What's wrong? Has something happened?"

Lottie hesitated. How was she supposed to tell him that she was torn between two men, and she didn't know how to handle it? That was not something she wanted to talk to Henry about, especially with his view on Oscar.

"It's…it's just work," she lied. "Things have been getting intense lately, and I'm just so tired."

Henry looked sympathetic. He reached out and rubbed her back. Lottie had to stop herself from leaning into him. Mostly because she needed to remain composed, and because she would fall off the stump she sat on.

"It sounds like you need a holiday," he said gently. "But that's not something you can afford, is it?"

"Not without losing my job in the process," Lottie muttered. "Mrs Leonard is lovely, but I doubt even she would let me have a few days off just like that. We need the work, after all."

"I know. We're not lucky enough to have the time to take off and do what we want." Henry sighed and shrugged. "Maybe someday that will happen. Just not today."

"I suppose." Lottie looked at him. "And what about you? You look more exhausted than I am. What have you been doing?"

"I've just been doing a lot of work at night. I'm going to places in the middle of the night to get something to report on."

"Dangerous work?"

Henry waggled his hand in the air.

"Maybe, maybe not."

Lottie groaned.

"Don't talk like that, Henry. You know that I don't like it when you do that."

"And I know you're not keen on having me discuss my more dangerous escapades for the newspaper," Henry countered. "I'm trying to keep it out of our conversations."

"It's not like that," Lottie protested. She turned on the stump enough to face him. "I'm just worried that something might happen to you. I don't want you getting hurt."

Henry blinked. He looked surprised that she would be concerned about him.

"You...you really mean that?"

"Did you think I wasn't going to care about you?"

"Well, given you've had your attention wavering elsewhere..."

Lottie groaned.

"You're talking about Oscar again, aren't you?"

"It's true, though, isn't it? Ever since he turned up, you're going out with him and experiencing things you could never do with me." Henry's tone took on a bitter note. "You're starting to pull away from everyone, including me, because of that man."

"That's not true!"

"It feels like it."

Lottie didn't want to have this argument with him as well. Not after Mrs Moore's words. She got to her feet and began to pace.

"What is it with everyone thinking they can decide things for me? Why can't I decide what to do on my own?"

"Lottie..."

"No, you listen to me!" She swung around on him. "If you don't like that I've made acquaintances with someone else, that's your prerogative. But I can't have my social circle so small that it's embarrassing. There's nothing wrong with getting to know other people. It's a different perspective, and it can be exciting."

"That's the problem." Henry stood up, his expression stony. "It's exciting, and I know you're someone who can get swept up when you're interested. You get really focused, which is admirable in the right situations."

"And you're saying this isn't a right situation?"

"Oscar Preston is mysterious, and when you know nothing about him..."

Lottie threw her hands up in the air with a frustrated cry.

"What is it with you and Mrs Moore? Both of you sound like you're trying to stop me being friends with Oscar. Nothing's happening, and if it does, that's my business not yours."

Henry's jaw tightened. Lottie hated making him feel awful, and she wanted to comfort him, but she needed to stand firm. She was always looking out for everyone else. Now she needed to concentrate on herself for once.

"We're just worried about you, that's all, Lottie."

"Do you trust me?" Lottie argued.

"What?"

"Just answer the question, Henry. Do you trust me?"

"Of course I do," Henry answered in bewilderment. "I've never let that waver at all."

"Then trust me to know what I'm doing. If I find out that he's wrong for me and I need to keep my distance, I'll make that decision. Your opinions can be there, but I need to figure things out on my own." Lottie absently tugged at her hair. "Choices were taken out of my hands many times in the past. Now I need to do it myself."

"I understand that." He ran his fingers through his hair. "I'm sorry, I just…I worry about you. I've been doing it for years, and seeing you pull away from me…"

"I'm not pulling away, Henry." Lottie approached him and took his hands. "I wouldn't do that. You're always going to be there, no matter what."

Something passed across Henry's face, and then it was gone. He swallowed.

"Do you mean that?" he whispered.

"Of course. You mean so much to me, and that's never going to change. Why would I walk away from all of that after what you've done? You're important to me."

They stared at each other. Then Henry leaned his forehead against hers with a heavy sigh.

"You have no idea how relieved I am to hear that," he said huskily. "To know something could happen to you…"

"Nothing's going to happen to me. I'm always going to be there."

Henry put his arms around her and hugged her, almost a little too tightly.

"I hope you're right," she heard him whisper.

CHAPTER 8

"Are you always going to be a seamstress?" Oscar asked as he and Lottie walked through the park. "You're going to sit in a shop and sew clothes for a living?"

"Why not? I enjoy it. It's hard work, but I do like it."

"Even though it is going to make your fingers incredibly sore when you're older?"

Lottie shrugged.

"It's better than what I did in the orphanage. I was splitting bits of rope into yarn. That cut my fingers up, especially during the winter. This is nothing compared to what I did before."

"Wouldn't you want to do a job that was more beneficial towards you?" Oscar frowned at her. "Because, in my opinion, being a seamstress doesn't seem like a job you can benefit from except to make other people look pretty."

Lottie blinked at him. Where was this coming from?

"But I like my job," she protested. "It gives me a feeling of satisfaction knowing that someone likes my work. It's not a problem for me to have that as my work for the rest of my life. I'd be content with it."

"Even though you barely get any time off and you'd be struggling to earn money for the rest of your life?"

"Not necessarily. I might get a commission to be a part of the Queen's dressmaker's circle. Or someone in the royal family."

Oscar snorted and shook his head as if it was a stupid suggestion.

"I very much doubt that's going to happen."

Lottie felt a flash of annoyance. She pulled away and turned to him, hands on her hips.

"Why do you think that?" she demanded. "Don't you think I'm capable enough of doing it?"

"Oh, I think you're very capable, but you're not using your full potential, are you?" Oscar held up a hand in apology. "I'm sorry that what I said came out the wrong way. I don't want you to think that I'm talking down to you."

"You did a little bit," Lottie muttered. "But why are you so interested in my job and if I should continue or not?"

Oscar tilted his head to one side and regarded her thoughtfully. Lottie felt a flutter in her stomach as he looked her over. He was like this whenever they went out. He would watch her as if she was a rare animal that he had the honour of treasuring. There was something in the way he treated her that made Lottie want to spend more time in his company. She felt pleased being in his presence, knowing that he was paying her attention.

The thought of Henry would pop into her mind, but Lottie pushed it away. Somehow, thinking about him while she was walking out with Oscar made her feel guilty. She didn't want that while she was trying to figure out why she was drawn to the pair of them.

It was not a position that she thought she would ever be in, and yet it was happening.

"I think I might have something for you that you will like, Lottie," Oscar said finally, his tone thoughtfully. "I'm sure you'll be happy to hear about it."

"How can you assume that when I haven't heard anything about it? Maybe it would be better if you told me what you're talking about."

"I have a job for you."

It took a moment for Lottie to realise what he had just said. Her jaw dropped, and she stared at him like he had gone mad.

"I beg your pardon. A job?"

"Don't look at me like that, Lottie. You don't need to worry about it."

"What am I supposed to do when you tell me that without any preamble?" Lottie folded her arms. "What sort of job would it be, anyway?"

"You'd work with me." Oscar stepped towards her, using that smile of his that made Lottie feel like her insides were melting. "I want you to become my secretary."

Lottie wondered if she was hearing him correctly. He chuckled, tapping the finger on the nose.

"You should see your expression right now. It's so adorable."

"Are you serious, Oscar?" Lottie gasped. "You want *me* to become your secretary?"

"Of course."

"But I don't have experience as a secretary. Wouldn't that be a problem?"

Oscar shrugged.

"So what? Everyone's got to start from somewhere, don't they? Might as well begin from the bottom, and being a secretary isn't all that difficult, especially if you're a fast learner." He took her hands, his gloves soft against her skin. "And from what I know of you, Lottie, you're a quick learner. You can adapt to any sort of situation."

"I don't know about that…"

"You've managed to adapt with everything since you were born. You wouldn't have survived as long as you did if you didn't. You're strong and resilient, and I admire that."

"You do?" Lottie whispered.

He leaned in, his face inches from hers. His breath tickled her mouth, and it caused Lottie to gasp.

"Oh, I absolutely do."

Was he going to kiss her? Lottie felt a thrill shoot through her body. Was this going to be her first kiss? But before that happened, Oscar suddenly pulled away, leaving her swaying and almost falling into him.

"And I think you would be perfect as my secretary. We just need to get you some nicer clothes to be appropriate for the position, but that's about it."

"I can't afford…" Lottie began, but he cut her off.

"I'll pay for everything. You don't need to worry about that at all." He grinned and winked, adjusting his hat. "As far as I'm concerned, when I'm around you have absolutely nothing to worry about."

Lottie believed that. A little bit. There was a bit of her, underneath the joy that she would be getting a new job, that told her something wasn't quite right. It was niggling away at her, almost annoying. But she pushed it aside, telling herself that this was just an opportunity that had come around for her, and she needed to grab onto it.

Oscar was showing her how to do that, and he believed in her. Lottie wanted him to be proud. Taking a deep breath, she smiled back.

"I'd like to know more about this position. Would you mind telling me about it?"

He beamed and took her arm.

"Of course. Why don't we get a cup of tea at the cafe over there, and I can tell you all about it?"

* * *

LOTTIE'S HEART felt as light as her footsteps as she headed home. She couldn't believe this was happening. She was going to be having something different in her life, something that would bring in more money. Oscar had said a secretary got paid a lot more than a seamstress, especially if the employer was wealthy, and there were also holidays off, not to mention she had more reasonable working hours.

It felt perfect. And she would get to see Oscar every day, working outside his office and taking notes while carrying out his requests. She couldn't wait to see him more than she already did.

Was she falling in love with him? Lottie had contemplated this a few times in recent days, unsure of the feelings she had whenever she was in Oscar's presence. Did it mean she was in love with him or what he brought with him? She didn't want to start expressing her feelings before she knew what was going on.

And why did they make her feel guilty?

It was sunset by the time Lottie returned home, and she was humming to herself as she let herself in.

"Mrs Moore?" she called. "I'm back!"

There was no response. Then Lottie remembered that her landlady went out every Thursday evening to spend time with her friends. They often went to a little restaurant nearby and ate dinner before playing cards. People raised eyebrows at the fact they were playing cards so openly, even if it was for fun, but it kept them happy. Mrs Moore liked causing confusion when it appeared they were gambling out in public; she thought it was amusing, and so did her friends.

They were just as eccentric as her, and Lottie loved that for them.

But there was movement coming from the sitting room. Was someone in the house? Lottie immediately felt on guard and wondered if she should run back out again. If someone was robbing them, she didn't want to get caught and attacked.

Then a shadow appeared in the doorway, and Lottie slumped against the door in relief.

"Henry! Don't scare me like that!"

"I'm sorry. I thought you'd be home by now." Henry frowned at her. "I know it was your day off, and we arranged to go and have dinner tonight."

"We did?" Lottie was confused. "I remember saying we should do that sometime, but did we actually arrange a day for it?"

"I thought we had." Henry's frown turned into a scowl. "It seems like you forget everything when you're around Oscar Preston. You were with him, weren't you?"

Lottie groaned.

"I'm not doing this tonight, Henry. That's not fair."

"What?"

"You're going to tell me that I shouldn't be around a man like him, that I should keep my distance because he's not good news."

Henry held up his hands.

"Slow down there. I wasn't going to say that."

"You didn't need to. Not with your way with words." Lottie pushed off the door and stalked towards him. "What I do with my free time is none of your business. It's not your job to chaperone me and tell me what I should be doing."

"Lottie…"

"It's not fair that I'm not allowed to do what I want because everyone keeps telling me otherwise. Oscar is a gentleman, and he's very nice to me. Why wouldn't I spend time with him?"

Henry folded his arms. He didn't look happy with this confrontation at all.

"I didn't come here to argue with you, Lottie. I thought you and I would be spending time together, and you weren't here. That's all."

Lottie snorted.

"You also wanted to tell me that I shouldn't trust Oscar. Just like every other time we talk about him."

"I don't do that!"

"You do!"

"Not last time," Henry pointed out. "I didn't do that when I found you in the park. We talked about anything else but him, if I recall."

"But you wanted to," Lottie shot back. "I don't know what your problem is with Oscar, but he's not the dangerous man you think he is. He's trustworthy enough."

"And how do you know that?"

"Because I trust him!"

Henry barked out a harsh laugh and turned away, pacing down the hall as he ran his hands through his hair, making it stand on end. Lottie found herself wanting to go to him and smooth down his hair, just to make him more presentable. Then she remembered that she was meant to be annoyed with him.

"That doesn't mean anything when he's less than trustworthy," Henry argued, his back still to her.

"How can you say that when you don't know him?"

"He's suddenly turning up, dressed smartly and being flirtatious with you, and offering you the finer things in life, and you're just lapping the attention up."

Lottie stared, wondering if she was hearing this correctly.

"It sounds like you're jealous of me having attention from someone else."

"What?" He turned around, looking stunned. "What are you talking about? Why would I be jealous?"

"Because I've found someone who isn't you to spend my time with, and you don't like it." Lottie glared at him. "We're friends, yes, but you need to trust me. I know what I'm doing."

"Do you?" Henry sounded like he was sneering. "Because I think you're still too naive when it comes to people."

"I don't think I'm naive!"

"You are when it comes to Oscar Preston. Something about him put me on edge, and if you were thinking properly, you would know what I'm talking about." Henry's eyes narrowed. "You're not someone who is taken in easily. Remember Fletcher at the orphanage? I had a bad feeling about him, and I know you did as well. I got that same feeling about Preston when we met."

Lottie couldn't believe it. Henry thought Oscar and Mr Fletcher were in the same category? She prodded him in the chest with her finger.

"Don't say things like that about Oscar! What did he ever do to you?"

"He's going to get you hurt if you carry on like this, Lottie."

"No, he isn't!"

"You don't know anything about him except he's wealthy!" Henry pointed out. "You're hurting yourself by seeing him continuously. One day, you'll find out he's bad news and you won't be able to do anything about it."

"You make it sound like he's going to take me away and put me into a brothel or something." Lottie barked out a laugh. "You've got a vivid imagination, Henry."

"I wouldn't be surprised if that did happen."

Lottie slapped him. Henry jerked, his expression shocked. Her fingers stung as she stepped back, her heart pounding.

"Don't talk about Oscar like that. I know you don't like him, but that's not an excuse to behave this way. You let me figure things out for myself, all right? Don't stick your nose in if I don't want it."

"Lottie..."

"Just leave, will you?" Lottie turned away. "I can't be around you right now. Not after you just insulted my intelligence. I had some good news, and you ruined it."

"Good news?" Henry started to follow her into the sitting room. "What good news?"

"Just get out, Henry. I'm not interested in talking to you about it anymore."

He looked as if he was going to argue with her, but he didn't, much to Lottie's surprise. He just looked at her with an expression that made her want to rush over and apologise to him before turning away and moving out of sight. As he left, Lottie felt a rush of cold go through her, and she started after him.

"Henry…"

But she didn't get any further before she heard the front door open and close sharply. Lottie sagged onto the settee and slumped over, staring at the floor. She couldn't believe a good day had turned into a bad one. She hadn't wanted that.

Now she was more worried about Henry than anything else. If only she could go after him and just apologise.

But she didn't think she could do that.

CHAPTER 9

"Thank you for the tea earlier, Lottie," Oscar said with a smile as he left his office. "That was very much needed."

Lottie looked up and gave him a smile in return.

"You're welcome, Mr Preston. Are you off to lunch now?"

"Yes, Mr Morgan and I are going to be heading over to that restaurant across the street." Oscar nodded at the tall, slim gentleman beside him before putting his hat on. "We won't be long. If any letters arrive, just leave them on my desk."

"Of course."

With another last look at her and a smile that made Lottie's heart flutter, Oscar led Mr Morgan out of Lottie's office. She still couldn't get over the fact that she was calling a big room like this her office. It was smaller than the room Oscar had, but it was all hers.

She couldn't believe this was her life now. She had been working as Oscar's secretary for almost two months, and it felt like an absolute dream. Lottie had shorter days, time to have a break, and she even had weekends off. It was better than being a seamstress. She did miss that job, and Mrs Leonard had been sad to see her go, but this was a better opportunity for her. Oscar was right: the job was easy to pick up and she had learned her position very quickly.

It was fun. And she got to be with Oscar almost every day. When he wasn't entertaining clients, he would take her out to lunch, or even in the evenings, giving her the finest food that had ever passed her lips. Lottie was sure she was going to get fat with such divine food passing her lips.

Mrs Moore was surprised that she had taken on such a position, but she hadn't shown her objections as Henry had done. She had been supportive, albeit a little dubious. Lottie could tell that she was concerned, but after their talk about having two men vying for her affections, she had kept quiet. It was as if she knew it was a sensitive subject.

Lottie didn't care, though. She got to be around Oscar, and she had better pay. She was able to save up more than she anticipated, and that was what she needed.

It had been years since she had seen her little brother, and Lottie missed him every day. She wanted to see him, to know he was safe and alive. But she had no idea where to start. If she had more money, maybe she could hire someone to find him. She had contemplated asking Oscar for help, but she couldn't bring herself to burden him that way. And she had a feeling she knew what Oscar was going to say: it was in the past, just leave it there.

She wasn't about to leave that.

"Excuse me?"

A young lad aged about eleven with a dirty face, but a smart black uniform was in the doorway, clutching a sack in his hands. Lottie had seen him before; he worked with the postmaster in the little post office down the street. She got up from her chair and walked around the desk, giving him a smile.

"Hello...Harry, isn't it?"

"Yes, miss." Harry wiped a grimy hand across his nose. "I've got some letters for Mr Preston. Mr Simmons said they needed to be delivered immediately."

"Of course. Mr Preston is gone for lunch, but I'll make sure he gets them."

Although Lottie wasn't too comfortable about having to handle letters that had been touched by Harry's clearly sticky fingers. He must have been having some sweets on the way over, or he had a cold that he was spreading to everyone else. With the epidemics lately due to the bad water, Lottie didn't want to end up sick herself.

Harry dug into the bag and withdrew a stack of letters, which she took, surprised at the amount.

"That's a lot of letters today."

"Mr Preston must be very popular," Harry replied, adjusting his hat. "I'll head off now, miss. Have a good day."

"You, too, Harry."

The boy left, and Lottie went into Oscar's office. He had said before that she could go into his office when he wasn't there, but she wasn't to touch anything on his desk. Apparently, the paperwork was sensitive, and he didn't want it to be disturbed. Lottie respected that. All she did, for the most part, was write letters dictated by Oscar and send them off as well as doing several errands. They were mundane enough, almost as if he was writing to family members. Lottie wanted to ask about that, but she decided against it. If Oscar wanted to tell her, then he would. She trusted him enough.

Mostly.

She went into the office, absently looking through the letters. They looked to be invitations, for the most part. A couple seemed to be important, and she put them at the top. Oscar wanted to pay attention to what was more important first, then he could get it out of the way. He had a particular way of doing things.

Then she noticed a letter in a cream-coloured envelope. The writing looked familiar, something niggling in the back of

Lottie's head. She was certain she had seen it before. Turning it over, she saw the return address.

It was the east end orphanage where she had been put. Lottie would never forget that place, even years later. It made her feel cold remembering that horrible place.

And that was why she recognised the handwriting. It was from Mr Fletcher. Lottie had seen it often enough to know.

She felt lightheaded, and Lottie stumbled against the desk, knocking his ink bottle over. Panicking, she dropped the letters and snatched the bottle up, grabbing at the blotting paper and trying to clear it up. Thankfully, it hadn't gone onto any of the documents that were on the desk itself, but now there was a nasty black stain on the wood.

Oscar was going to be upset. Even though it was an accident, she would end up feeling very guilty and he wouldn't be happy with her at all. Things had to be neat and tidy, and she had just messed things up.

Her heart still pounding while clutching the ink bottle, she sagged onto the floor, leaning her head against the cold wood. This was going to be difficult to explain and apologise for. Then she realised something. What was the bottle doing out of the well? It was a strange thing for it to be elsewhere except where it was supposed to be.

Had Oscar taken it out for some reason and not put it back? That was possible. Should she put it back?

Getting to her feet, she put the bottle down where she had seen it and started to gather the letters. It was only then that she saw her hands were black and they were staining the envelopes. Embarrassed, she tossed them haphazardly onto the desk and hurried from the room. She needed to wash her hands and get the ink off before it stained.

She was still stuck in her thoughts as she left her office, and she didn't see the man coming in at the same time. They collided, and Lottie gasped as she almost lost her balance.

"Careful!" Hands grabbed her elbows. "What's the rush?"

Lottie felt the air leave her body in a rush when she saw Henry standing before her. She had never seen such a welcoming sight like this before.

"Henry!" She leaned her head on his chest. "You scared me!"

"I can tell. You were clearly not paying attention." Henry eased her back and stared at her. Then he saw her hands. "What's happened to you? What have you been doing?"

"I need to wash my hands," Lottie gasped, realising that she was struggling to breathe properly. "I...I saw something that... that..."

"Slow down, Lottie." Henry pressed his hands on her shoulders. "Take a deep breath and let it out slowly. Keep doing that until you calm down. You won't be able to talk if you're panicking."

Lottie wanted to snap back that she knew that, but she couldn't bring herself to talk when she was unable to draw a breath without her chest hurting. Closing her eyes, she leaned into Henry and forced herself to slow her breathing. It took a while, but soon she was able to think more clearly without her mind going mad. She looked up at Henry, who gave her a gentle smile and brushed his fingers across her cheek.

"Better?"

"A little." Lottie leaned into his hand, grateful for the warmth. "What are you doing here? I thought you were busy with work."

"I found out something I thought you would want to know. But I think you need to talk to me first." He cupped her cheek in her hand. "What's gotten you spooked that you're white as a sheet? What happened?"

Lottie needed to tell someone. She needed to be sure that she wasn't going mad. She swallowed.

"I need to clean my hands first," she croaked. "And then I need something to drink."

It was a shame she couldn't have something stronger right now.

* * *

"You think Fletcher's been writing to Preston?" Henry said in a stunned voice as Lottie tried not to gulp down her tea.

"I'm pretty sure it was his handwriting. I've seen it often enough. And it was from the orphanage." Lottie shuddered. "I just…I don't know, something cold washed over me. Just thinking about him and what he had planned for me…"

"You were lucky to get out when you did," Henry grunted, sipping his own tea. "What I don't understand is why he's writing to Preston. What connection do they have?"

"I don't know, but the thoughts running through my head are not good." Lottie shook her head. "I can't believe Oscar would even be acquainted with Mr Fletcher. He must know that he's a bad person."

"Maybe he doesn't. It's a possibility that he thinks Mr Fletcher is just a normal person." Henry raised his eyebrows. "You do know that not everyone is aware of Mr Fletcher's… activities. He might have had connections, but it's not like he was going to put them on display with what he was up to. Nobody would want to willingly associate with someone who is happy to exploit young women for their own means."

He did have a point. Lottie couldn't see Oscar being friends with Mr Fletcher. They were far too far apart in terms of social standing and personalities. He was also aware of what happened to Lottie at the orphanage and why she had run away. So why was Mr Fletcher writing to him? It didn't make any sense.

This was giving her a headache.

Then she remembered that Henry had come to her for something. Trying to ignore the burning in her mouth, she added another sugar to the tea and stirred it. She needed something to sweeten her drink right now.

"What was it you wanted to see me about? You don't normally come and meet me at Oscar's offices. You tend to keep away."

Henry's jaw tightened, his eyes narrowed.

"I have my reasons for staying away. I'm not about to get accused of not trusting you, Lottie..."

Lottie groaned.

"You still remember that?"

"I wasn't about to forget the moment you slapped me for the first time, was I?" Henry glanced away. "You said you didn't want me hovering over you, and I respected that."

Lottie regarded him and saw how withdrawn from her Henry seemed to be. It was shocking how he could change in just a few months, and Lottie didn't like it. She wanted her old friend. She needed to have Henry back.

"It's been so strange not seeing you around," she whispered. "I've missed you, Henry."

Henry cleared his throat, not meeting her gaze.

"I had to come and see you this time. I found something I thought you would want to know about."

"Like what?" Lottie sat up. "Have you found Billy? Is it about him?"

"Well, not quite."

"What does that mean?"

"Is this her?"

Lottie stiffened when she heard the voice behind her. She turned and saw the short, buxom woman with greying hair pulled back in a bun wearing a dark brown dress. She looked nervous, watching the pair apprehensively.

It didn't take much for Lottie to recognise her. Her memory was sharp when it came to this woman. She stared in stunned amazement.

"Amy?"

Amy smiled. The sight of a familiar face made Lottie almost burst into tears. Jumping up, she hurried over to the woman and flung her arms around her. They embraced, and suddenly there were a lot of tears.

"Oh, my goodness. Let me look at you." Amy eased her back and looked Lottie up and down, tears streaming down her cheeks. "I can't believe you're all grown up now. You are so lovely."

"Thanks," Lottie mumbled. She didn't know what else to say to that. It felt strange. She absently brushed herself down. "How...how did Henry find you? Were you still at the orphanage?"

Amy shook her head.

"No, I wasn't. After what happened with you running away, Fletcher..."

Lottie stiffened.

"What did he do?"

"Why don't you come and sit down?" Henry suggested, standing up and pulling out a chair between him and Lottie's place. "It might be easier for us. And do you want some tea, Amy?"

"If you wouldn't mind?" Amy gave him a shy smile as she sat down. "I know you said we were going to see Lottie, but the nerves that have come over me are something I haven't experienced in a long time."

"Why?" Lottie couldn't help but ask. "Did you think I didn't want to see you?"

"Well, it's been a long time." Amy absently smoothed out her skirts. "Anything could happen."

She did have a point. But Lottie knew she could never be upset with Amy. The woman had done her best to look after her and Billy, and did what she could to help her escape. She felt bad for not getting Amy to come with her, but that wouldn't have happened. The woman had loved her job.

Although, from the way she was speaking, that was likely not a possibility anymore.

Henry came back with another cup of tea, placing it in front of Amy. She added two sugars into the tea and stirred it quickly, the spoon clinking against the sides. Her hand trembled a little as she took a sip.

"Fletcher was furious when you ran away. He reported me to the warden and said that I couldn't be trusted to be around children if I was going to let them get away all the time. The warden...well, he agreed, and I was thrown out of the orphanage."

Lottie gasped.

"I...I'm so sorry, Amy. It was my fault..."

"You don't need to worry about it. I knew what was happening, and I'm not ashamed of what I did." Amy sipped her tea. "I'm just upset that I wasn't allowed to take Billy with me. He was taken away and I didn't see him again."

Lottie sat forward.

"So do you know where Billy is?"

"Given his age, he's likely gone out to a factory or a farm somewhere to work." Amy shrugged. "He'd be sixteen now, so he would have been sent out to work even if he were a favoured child."

She did have a point. The oldest child at the orphanage had been fourteen. They became old enough that they were sent out for manual labour. If any of the children were lucky enough to leave before then, it would be for jobs such as chimney sweep or other apprenticeship jobs that made Lottie's stomach churn. It was nothing short of a miracle that she hadn't been put to work as Mr Fletcher had wanted.

"Where do you think he is now?" she asked.

"I have no idea, love. I wish I did." Amy looked at Henry. "I've been working as a companion for an elderly lady since I left the orphanage. She was kind enough to look after me when I was trying to find another job. She's since passed away, and left me some money to let me live comfortably for the rest of my life. Something I never thought would happen."

"But how...?" Lottie looked at Henry. "How did you find her?"

"I have a few contacts, and I asked my employer at the printing shop if he knew where Amy might have gone." Henry's expression was slightly smug. "He was fond of Amy, and they talked often. Turns out, he was the one who got Amy the job. He pointed me in her direction."

"I will always be grateful for that man's help," Amy chimed in with a smile. "I think I would've ended up in the workhouse if I couldn't find myself anything. There are so many people in London but not as many jobs to go around. And if there are jobs, they're not enough for me to earn my way. Just enough to get some bread and not much else."

Lottie knew all about that. She had been doing that when she was ten years old and then resorted to stealing because it wasn't enough. It had been hard enough when she was a child, and she couldn't begin to think how it would be for an adult.

"Where do you think Mr Fletcher put Billy?" Lottie looked from Henry to Amy and back again. "Is there a chance that he was the one who sent him elsewhere? As punishment for me running away?"

"I think he would do that. You know how mean that man is." Amy sighed. "But I wouldn't know where he'd put him. Fletcher has a lot of contacts."

A stab of frustration hit Lottie in the gut. She couldn't believe they were this close, and then there was nothing. Henry leaned over and took her hand.

"You don't have to fret so much, Lottie. We'll find him. You know I'll be able to find him."

And that Lottie knew. She trusted Henry to look after her, to make sure she had what she wanted. Amy chuckled.

"I figured you two would end up together in the end. It's nice to see you furthering yourself in ways better than I thought possible."

"But we're not...together..." Lottie faltered, but Amy kept talking.

"I was worried about what happened to you, Lottie. But I knew you were resourceful. You wouldn't have let an opportunity slide. And you look great. Things have been looking up for you, haven't they?"

Lottie bit her lip, glancing at Henry. His expression clouded a little, and he sat back, his hand sliding off hers.

"They certainly have," he murmured.

"Anyway, Lottie, why don't you tell me what's been going on with your life?" Amy took Lottie's hand, her fingers warm through her gloves. "I want to know how you managed to grow into this stunning woman before me."

CHAPTER 10

"I can't believe you managed to find Amy." Lottie looked at Henry as they walked down the street. "I didn't think it would be possible."

"Well, it's possible, and I thought you would want to see her again." Henry grinned. "Did it work? Did that make you happy?"

"I'm very happy. I missed her so much." Lottie sighed. "I just wish I had better news about Billy. I want to see him."

"I know. But we'll find him. We'll find someone who knows where he is." He rubbed the back of his neck. "I doubt we can ask Fletcher about it, though. It's far too dangerous, and then he'll know where you are."

Lottie shuddered. She didn't want to ever encounter Mr Fletcher again. Not after what happened.

But if they had to, they would. Lottie would do anything to find Billy. She wanted to see her little brother again. It had been far too long.

She absently kicked at a stone on the pavement, sending it skittering into the road as a carriage passed by, the rumbling noise loud in her ears. Lottie resisted the urge to clamp her hands over her ears. It was making her head hurt.

LOTTIE - THE RUNAWAY

"Lottie?" Henry slowed to a stop. "What's wrong? You're looking...I don't know, not quite yourself."

"I thought I was doing fine."

"How long have I known you? There's something different, and it's not happiness that you've been reunited with Amy."

Lottie sighed, rubbing her hands over her face. She felt like she was going to be sick. Knowing that they had a chance to find Billy and they still had no idea where he was sent things into a spin inside her. She hated this feeling.

"I just want my brother back, that's all. I haven't seen him for such a long time."

"I know."

"He should have come with me. We should have run away together. But he tackled Fletcher instead and made sure I got away. Even with everything, he was thinking of me." Lottie could feel her eyes stinging, and she squeezed them shut tight. "I should have gone back for him. I should have returned the favour. And yet..."

Henry didn't say anything. He turned her around and pulled her into his arms. Lottie leaned into him, wrapping her arms around him as her head rested on his chest. It was then that she let the tears fall, and she began to sob. Henry slowly rubbed her back, resting his chin on the top of her head.

"It's all right," he whispered. "It's going to be all right. You'll see your brother again. Billy's out there, and he's waiting for you."

"Why do I get the feeling I'm never going to see him again?" Lottie whimpered. "What if...?"

"Don't think about the what ifs. You'll see him again." Henry cupped her head in his hands and urged her to look up at him. His eyes were piercing as he captured her gaze. "Even if he died because of something, there will be a grave. Doesn't matter if he's alive or dead, I will find him. I'm good at finding people, and I'll do that for you."

Lottie swallowed back the hard lump building in her throat.

Tears tickled her cheeks, and her nose felt thick with the mucus blocking it. She tried to breathe through her mouth.

"You promise that?"

Henry nodded.

"I promise. When it comes to you, I will not break that promise."

She wasn't prepared the kiss, and suddenly Lottie couldn't breathe. She pulled away quickly and fumbled for her handkerchief.

"I...I'm sorry." Henry stuttered over his words. "I didn't mean..."

"Just wait a moment." Lottie blew her nose, and then she put her handkerchief back in her pocket. "I just couldn't breathe, that's all."

"And what...?"

"Do that again." Lottie stepped towards him, her hands on his chest. "I want you to do that again."

Henry looked stunned, as if he didn't quite believe what happened. Then he cupped her cheek and kissed her again. This time, Lottie kissed him back. She felt warm and safe, wrapped in his arms and hugging him close. She had no idea how long it lasted, standing there on the pavement in the growing dusk, but she didn't care if anyone saw them. She just wanted to be in Henry's arms for longer.

They were both breathless when they broke the kiss, Henry's cheeks flushed and his eyes bright. He swallowed.

"I...I didn't think you were ever going to let me do that."

"Why not?"

"Well..."

Lottie knew what he was going to say. Because of Oscar. He thought she would have saved it for him. She held up a hand.

"I don't want to talk about him, Henry. Leave it be. Please?"

Henry didn't answer for a moment, his expression shifting to one that made her uncomfortable. She didn't want the mood to be ruined between them, not right now. She wanted to reach for him, to comfort him and assure him she wasn't going anywhere. But with everything going on, she found that she couldn't promise that.

"Let's get you home." Henry held out an arm. "I'll make sure you return to Mrs Moore without any further problems."

"I can't believe I managed to get the afternoon off," Lottie said as they continued again down the street. "And I'm glad I did because I could spend more time with Amy."

"She certainly enjoyed it as well. I think this was more therapeutic for her than it was for you." Henry smiled, but it seemed more forced. "And she said she would do what she could to find Billy herself. She's got her own contacts. I think it could be just what we need."

"I hope we do manage to find him." Lottie paused. "Do you think we'll be able to press charges on Mr Fletcher or something? We could go to the police…"

"Do you think they're going to do anything about it? Especially when we have no definitive proof, and Fletcher is likely going to be believed more than you?"

"I could get Oscar…"

Henry growled.

"I don't want to hear his name. If he's exchanging correspondences with Fletcher, he's not going to be of any help. We're going to have to do this on her own."

"But how?"

"I've got a few ideas. You let me handle it."

Lottie fell silent. She shouldn't have mentioned Oscar's name, even though he had the connections to put the pressure on Mr Fletcher. But then she remembered the letter in his office and wondered if she could use that herself.

She needed to get back to the office to find out. That wasn't something she could discuss with Henry, though. He would either be all for breaking in, or he would tell her to leave it alone.

Either way, Lottie wasn't letting it go. She needed to get to that letter.

* * *

THE NEXT DAY, Oscar was meant to be out for the day. He sent a letter to Lottie telling her that first thing in the morning, and he had given Lottie the day off. She could do what she wanted instead, but then she decided to make the most of his absence. The letter was still likely in the office, and she needed to find out what Mr Fletcher said.

Once she had her breakfast, Lottie bid Mrs Moore farewell as normal and headed to the office. The place was locked, but Lottie knew where the spare key was, tucked under the mat just outside the main door. She used it to slip into her office, and then into Oscar's. Her heart was pounding as she did so, looking around to make sure nobody had seen her sneaking in.

Oscar's office was on the same floor as a solicitors, and they had people coming in and out all the time. They might not be suspicious if Lottie, as Oscar's secretary, let herself in, but she had to be careful.

She closed the door behind her and went to the desk. The letters were still on top. They hadn't moved, as far as she could tell. So, Oscar hadn't noticed the ink stain on his desk just yet. Maybe she should make the most of this and try to clean it up. There was a chance that she could get rid of it.

Mr Fletcher's letter was on the top, untouched but with smudged fingers from the day before. She snatched it up and began to open it, her hands trembling. She couldn't believe that the man who tried to sell her to a questionable man was corresponding with Oscar, someone she was experiencing feelings for. How was it possible that he could mess her life up years down the line? It wasn't fair.

Then Lottie thought about what was going on between her,

Oscar, and Henry. She knew there were feelings for the pair of them, but it was not possible to have both in her life. If she chose one, she couldn't have the other around. That would be unfair on everyone. But it didn't matter which side she picked, someone was going to end up broken-hearted.

Henry loved her. Lottie could see that. He had always looked after her, and his love for her was coming through every day. Nobody needed to guess when he was around her how he felt, and it solidified it for Lottie after he kissed her the day before. She knew she had his heart.

And then there was Oscar. A man she was falling for as well, but she didn't know anything about him. Not anything meaningful, anyway. He kept things secretive, and while he treated her with lavish presents and taking her to see what she could have if she was of his social standing, it was all superficial. It was like Oscar was keeping himself protected from everyone, including her.

He gave her financial security, and he promised to give her anything she wanted. But Lottie didn't know if she could take it, even if it would be the more logical option. She didn't like thinking about Henry negatively, but she knew his position on the newspaper wouldn't be as secure as Oscar's current position. If she wanted a better life, choosing Oscar would be the option.

But if she wanted love, and knowing it was unconditional, it would be Henry. Lottie knew she would be happy with him, even if they weren't as financially secure.

The letter was open in her hands, but Lottie hadn't even read it yet. She had gone straight down to the signature, and saw it was from Mr Fletcher. So he really was writing to Oscar. But why?

Before she got a chance to read it all, she heard the outer-door opening. Panicking, she folded the letter and shoved that and her envelope into her pocket, grabbing a cloth from the top of the desk while snatching the ink bottle out of the well, dribbling a little on top of the old stain. Then she began to dab at the mess she had made the day before.

Her heart was pounding as the door opened, and Oscar came in. He stopped, his expression surprised.

"Lottie? What are you doing here? I thought you would be having the day off."

"I…I thought I'd finish off some work I hadn't completed yesterday." That would be true enough if he saw her desk. Lottie gestured at the mess. "I was putting things on your desk, and I accidentally knocked over your ink bottle."

Oscar frowned.

"But how can you do that when it was in the inkwell?"

"Believe me, I don't know how I managed it, either, but it was not in the inkwell, and I didn't notice, and then I knocked it over…"

Lottie had tried to pretend she was panicking, but then it was real. Oscar didn't like mess. Tears pricked at her eyes, and she tried to blink them back.

"I…I'm so sorry, Oscar. I didn't mean to make a mess…"

"It's all right." Oscar took the items from her hands and placed them on the desk. Then he tugged off his gloves, putting them into his pocket. "You made a mistake. We all do that."

He took her hands, and Lottie was shocked at how cold his hands were without the gloves. That was strange as they always felt warm with them on. What was wrong with her? Why was she noticing this now?

"I'm sorry…"

"You're not hurt, are you?"

Lotto frowned.

"No, of course not."

"Then no harm done." Oscar smiled. "We can clean it up. Or I can buy myself a new desk."

Lottie licked her lips. This was a better response than she thought, although she was scared about what was going to happen now. Oscar had always scolded her about cleanliness, saying he liked it that way, and now he was forgiving her for a big mess? Something didn't feel right.

"What are you doing here, anyway?" she asked. "I thought you said you would be out of the office today."

"I am. I just needed to collect something first. You didn't need to come in today, darling," he said. "You could have had the day off."

"I...I didn't want to leave my work as it was..." Lottie stopped. "Wait, did you just call me darling?"

"Why wouldn't I call you that?"

"Well, we're...we're not..."

"We're not courting or anything?" He finished for her. "Not like other couples?"

"I..." Lottie floundered. "I didn't realise we were a couple."

Oscar chuckled.

"What did you think the outings we had together were for? I thought we were courting."

"You never..."

"I never said anything about it. I thought it would've been obvious." Oscar leaned in and kissed her forehead. "I thought you'd know by now that I want you in my life more than just as my secretary."

Lottie didn't know what to say. Her mind had gone blank, and her cover seemed to have vanished. She stared at him as Oscar raised her hands to his mouth and kissed her fingers, his eyes never leaving her.

"Lottie Watson, my darling girl. Will you do me the honour of becoming my wife?"

CHAPTER 11

"You've just received a letter, Lottie," Mrs Moore said, entering the room. "It came just now."

Lottie frowned, putting her book aside as she took the letter from the widow. There was nothing on the envelope that suggested who it was from. She didn't recognize the handwriting, either.

"Do you know who it's from?" she asked.

"All I know is a young lad came by and said it was from a neighbour of his. That was all." Mrs Moore shrugged before sitting in her chair again "Maybe it's from your gentleman friend?"

Lottie was almost about to ask which one she was talking about, but then realised she meant Oscar. Even though she hadn't accepted the proposal just yet—she had asked to think about it once she had gotten over the shock—he kept sending flowers and letters of undying love to her house. She couldn't bring herself to go into work, knowing that she was going to meet him. He would be demanding an answer from her if she did.

And there was a chance she would end up seeing Mr Fletcher, and she wasn't about to let that happen. The thought of encountering that man again scared her. She knew it would be bad if they crossed paths once more, especially with the way Mr Fletcher was focused on her at the orphanage. Years might have passed, but she knew it wouldn't have waned. He would want to take her again.

She still couldn't understand why Oscar was interacting with him, even if it was through letters. It didn't make sense. Surely, he would know that it was a bad idea. But maybe he didn't know the truth behind the man's mask, although Oscar prided himself in knowing who a good person was or not.

Lottie had a feeling he didn't know the truth about Mr Fletcher. She should tell him. But if he did know…

That was going to break her heart knowing that someone she had grown feelings for was friends with a man like that.

"Well?" Mrs Moore prompted. "Are you going to open it or are you just going to stare at it and expect it to open on its own?"

"Oh!" Lottie turned the envelope over and opened it. "My mind was wandering."

"Is it another letter of love from your beau?"

Lottie grimaced at the word 'beau'.

"Please don't call him that, Mrs Moore. It's not like that."

"It must be an embarrassing situation if you're staying here and not going into work."

"Why embarrassing?"

Mrs Moore gave her a sympathetic smile.

"You might find him attractive, and you feel something for him, but it's not enough. You sense something in your gut that this isn't quite right, and you don't want to go back and look him in the eye." She pressed a hand over her heart. "In here, you don't want to marry him. It feels like it would be a mistake if you agree."

Lottie didn't know what to say to that for a moment. Was that how she felt? Did she believe that she wasn't in love enough to get married to Oscar? She hadn't thought about it like that. There were second thoughts, but to think it was about that...

She pushed that aside and opened the letter. After a few lines, she knew it wasn't from Oscar. She scanned it before reading it a second time.

"It's from Amy."

"Amy?"

"The woman who looked after me at the orphanage. She wants to meet me, says it's important, and I must see her as soon as I can."

Mrs Moore frowned.

"If it's important, why didn't she come here to talk to you? Anyone else would have done that?"

"I don't know, but I should go over and see what's going on. She sounds distraught." Apprehension prickled along the back of Lottie's neck. "Maybe she's seen Mr Fletcher and knows that he's nearby."

"Then wouldn't it be safer to stay here instead of going out? You don't want to run into him again, do you?"

That was the last thing Lottie wanted. She didn't want to be anywhere near the man if she could avoid it, and if this was about him, the idea of stepping outside the front door was terrifying. But Amy sounded scared, and her words implied that she needed to see her as soon as possible. Maybe she was thinking the same thing and didn't want to leave the house?

"I must go and make sure she's all right. Amy is my friend, and I don't think I can leave her alone as she is."

"You're going to go to her?"

"I'll have to if she won't come to me." Lottie stood up and left the room, picking her coat off the rack in the hall. "I don't know why she wouldn't write it to me, but it must be important if she wants to speak to me in person."

Mrs Moore hurried after her. She looked concerned, her

expression taut with worry as she watched Lottie shrug on her coat.

"Don't go alone," she pleaded. "It could be dangerous."

"What could be dangerous about seeing a friend?"

"With Oscar Preston's proposal, and this Fletcher being in the area, it would be best that you're not going around on your own."

Lottie sighed and squeezed the widow's hands.

"You don't have to worry about me. I've been able to keep myself safe all these years. This won't be any different."

"How can you be so calm about all of this?"

"Someone must be. And panicking isn't going to get me anywhere." Lottie buttoned up her coat. "Besides, she might have something on Billy. She said she would ask around and try to find something."

"I thought Henry was doing that for you. I know he was helping to look for him."

"He's not come up with anything just yet. Nothing solid, anyway. Maybe Amy has." Lottie put her hat on, checking it in the mirror. "I'll be right back. The address Amy gave me isn't far. I'll return as soon as I can."

Mrs Moore still didn't look happy about it. She folded her arms and scowled.

"I really don't like this," she said. "Where are you going?"

Lottie wanted to tell her not to worry, but she could tell the woman wasn't about to let her go without being given what she wanted. Sighing, she handed the letter over.

"It's this place. It's not far from here, right?"

"No, so I'm going to give you thirty minutes to get there and return. If you're not back in thirty-five minutes, I'm coming to look for you."

Lottie sighed.

"Mrs Moore…"

"No, I'm not arguing with you on this, Lottie," Mrs Moore cut her off sharply. "With everything going on right now, I'd feel more comfortable knowing that you were safe. If you intend to go off like this, I want to be sure you'll be back."

Lottie felt like crying. Even after years of being under the wing of the woman who took her in, it was still strange to have someone looking after her and showing they cared. She bit her lip and nodded.

"All right. I promise." Then, on impulse, she suddenly hugged her. "Thank you."

"Now be careful." Mrs Moore stepped back and folded her arms. She didn't look happy. "I honestly don't know why I'm allowing this. I feel like I'm going to regret it."

Lottie didn't answer, letting herself out and shutting the door as quickly as she could. She had a feeling Mrs Moore would change her mind and keep her home if she waited around any longer.

* * *

AMY HAD ASKED to meet her at a park a few streets away, right on the corner. It was a place that Mrs Moore had told Lottie to keep away from as it was known for pickpockets and for where homeless people would spend their time. Not a place for a young lady to be. If Amy had asked to meet there, there had to be a reason.

She quickened her pace and hurried across the road to reach the park entrance. There didn't seem to be anyone around. Had she gotten here before Amy, or was Amy inside the park? It would be rather strange for someone as respectable as her friend to be in the park. Maybe she thought it would be somewhere they couldn't be overheard.

All Lottie knew was that Amy had information on Billy's disappearance, and she knew where he was. She wasn't about to pass up the opportunity to find her brother. She needed to get him back.

"Amy?" Lottie looked around. "Amy, where are you?"

"Lottie."

Amy stepped out from behind a tree lining the street. She looked sombre. Lottie hurried to her.

"What is it? What did you find out about Billy?"

"Run."

Lottie stopped. The word came a whisper, spoken through gritted teeth. Then she saw how scared Amy looked, her body tense. And the bruise on her cheek, swelling up under her eye. Lottie gasped.

"What happened to you? Who hurt you?"

"Run, Lottie," Amy pleaded, a tear rolling down her cheek. "Go home."

"I think that's a bit pointless now, Amy." Lottie froze when she heard a familiar voice. "Lottie's not going anywhere."

Her heart pounding, Lottie turned to see the man standing behind her. He must have come out of the park. He was now bald, and his face was thinner than she remembered, but there was no forgetting the evil-looking eyes and the smirk.

"Fletcher," Lottie whimpered.

"Hello, Lottie. It's been a long time." Mr Fletcher looked her up and down. "You're all grown up now. Very lovely. I knew you'd turn into a beauty."

"What..." Lottie stepped back as he moved towards her. "What's going on? What did you do to Amy?"

"I just showed her that she shouldn't have gone against me and my...clients. They weren't happy at all that you ran away with her help." Mr Fletcher glanced past her at Amy. "It's a shame that she's too old, otherwise she might have been a good consolation prize for them."

Lottie heard a noise come from Amy, but she didn't turn around. She was beginning to get some clarity on the situation she was in. How could this be happening now? Why didn't she take someone with her to go to meet Amy?

Mrs Moore was going to be disappointed with her.

Mrs Moore. She would be looking for her if Lottie didn't return.

"I don't know what you want with me," she said, holding up her hands as Mr Fletcher advanced on her. "But my landlady said she would come looking for me if I don't return soon. She will notify the police..."

"She's going to say nothing. Not once I have a word with her." Mr Fletcher grabbed her arm before Lottie could back up and pulled her to him, Lottie falling against his chest. "She won't say anything after that unless she wants to get into trouble herself. And then there will be nobody to save you from what we had planned for you years ago."

"You mean when you tried to sell a child for money?" Lottie spat. "I'm not a child anymore."

"Doesn't matter. You'll still fetch a good price." Mr Fletcher sniggered. "And as pretty as you are, it will be so easy to get even more."

Lottie felt sick. How was this even happening? She couldn't believe she had gotten herself into this position. She tried to pull away, but he wouldn't let go.

"There's no point in getting away from me. I know where you live, after all."

"I'm not going anywhere with you!"

He smirked, and Lottie's gut rolled at the smell coming from his breath. He looked past her at Amy with a steely gaze.

"You'd better get out of here now," he snarled. "Unless you want me to deal with you as well."

"You said you wanted to talk to her," Amy protested. "You didn't say you would..."

"And you believed me?" Mr Fletcher scoffed. "You're always looking for the best in people, even with me. Lottie ran away years ago, and I lost out on a lot of money. But this time, she's not getting away."

"No!" Lottie tried to yank her arm away. "Let me go!"

LOTTIE - THE RUNAWAY

"Stop it!" Amy started forward. "This isn't right"

"Oh, shut up!"

With his attention on Amy, Lottie took her chance. She stamped hard on his foot, which made him grunt and his grip loosened on her arm. Taking that opportunity, Lottie rammed her elbow into his stomach. Mr Fletcher let out a gasp and collapsed to the ground, clutching at his middle. Not looking to see what Amy was doing; Lottie began to run. She had to get back to the house. If she was with Mrs Moore, then she would feel safe.

Or maybe she should go and find Henry. He often worked late at the paper. She could go there instead.

Darting around the corner, her heart pounding in her chest, Lottie collided with someone, and it knocked the air out of her. Hands grabbed her arms as she wobbled.

"Where's the fire here?"

Was she imagining things? Why was he here? Lottie looked up and saw Oscar watching her with a lazy smile. She felt the relief start, only to stop when she remembered the letter from Mr Fletcher. Then panic began to replace the relief.

No, she couldn't see him as a saviour. He was a part of this. Lottie knew he had to be involved with this mess. Did he also put his hands on Amy as well to get her to cooperate?

"Why don't you go back and talk to Mr Fletcher?" Oscar suggested, giving her a smile that didn't reach his eyes as he began to back her up. "I know he's been looking forward to a reunion with you, so it would be impolite for you to run away?"

"You...you know what would've happened to me..." Lottie was struggling to breathe, still trying to comprehend what was going on. "I told you..."

"And you think that means you're going to be safe now you're away from it?" Oscar sniggered. "How do you think Fletcher had the contacts to sell the many girls that came across his path? He wouldn't have gotten them on his own. And the cut I get is incredibly generous."

Lottie felt like she was going to pass out. How was this happening to her now? She hadn't anticipated he would be an active participant.

"Run, Lottie!" Amy's shout got her attention. "Get out of here!"

There was a cry and what could have been a thunderclap.

"Shut up, woman!" Mr Fletcher snarled. "Preston, where's the girl? I'm not waiting any longer."

"She's right here."

"No!" Lottie pushed him in the chest, making him stumble back. "Keep away from me!"

"Lottie, don't…"

She ducked under his arm and started to run. If she could find someone, anyone, walking down the street, she would be able to get help. But with the park full of undesirables, people kept to their homes and didn't come out unless they absolutely had to. They probably thought she was one of them as well. Lottie felt sick knowing that there would likely be nobody to help her.

She could hear Oscar shouting her name, and she glanced back to see him charging after her, a look of rage on his face. The mask she had seen on him had slipped, and now she was seeing the real person.

He would catch up with her, so she was going to have to play this smartly. It had been a long time since she ran away from someone.

Taking a sharp left, she ran into the park.

CHAPTER 12

The park was overgrown, and everything seemed to be in a state of disarray. Nobody wanted to come here when they were aware of the people who frequented the place. But if it was in a mess, it meant more places to hide.

She was a lot bigger than when she was running away before, but it would be enough.

Checking that Oscar wasn't behind her to see, Lottie jumped off the path and scrambled under a bush. She knew this would ruin her clothes, but she would worry about that later. The bush was prickly and kept scraping at her skin. She gritted her teeth to stop herself from crying out in pain, lying on her stomach and keeping as low as she could without burying her face into the dirt. She was under the bush far enough that, even with the uncut grass, she wouldn't be seen.

Hopefully, there wouldn't be a clue that she was hiding here. Her clothes weren't bright, which was a relief. If anything, she looked like she could blend in with her surroundings.

"Lottie!"

Her heart pounded in her chest at the sound of Oscar's voice. Then she saw a pair of legs appear through the gap in the bush.

He was so close, and Lottie held her breath. She was scared that he would look around and see her, even in her hiding place.

Oscar growled and muttered something under his breath. Then another pair of legs appeared, slowing from a jog and a gasping of air.

"Where is she?" Mr Fletcher asked between gulps.

"She's gone," Oscar replied grimly. "She's faster than I thought."

"Or she could be hiding."

Lottie's heart almost stopped. She wasn't going to get caught like this. She wouldn't, but she couldn't move. They would hear her, and there were two of them now. She would be trapped if she wasn't careful.

"This park is going to turn into a maze," Oscar grumbled. "We're not likely to find her with all of this. That girl is resourceful, if nothing else."

"And very slippery," Mr Fletcher agreed. "I should've grabbed her and knocked her out when I had the chance."

"Where's the woman?"

"I gave her a slap and told her she was to wait where she was. She's not going anywhere."

Oscar snorted.

"She was the one who helped the girl flee the first time. She might've been forced into this now, but that's not going to last for long."

"Well, what do we do, then?" Mr Fletcher demanded. "We're going to lose out on a lot of money for her! And it's bigger than it was years ago."

"You think I don't know that? I was the one who saw her in the street, and I've spent weeks getting her to trust me. I even proposed to her so she wouldn't run away!"

Mr Fletcher scoffed at that.

"Well, maybe you should've turned the charm on a little bit more," he sneered. "Because she is far too clever. She knew that

LOTTIE - THE RUNAWAY

there was something wrong with you, and that's why she was pulling away."

"Maybe you shouldn't have written to me when you knew she was going to be my secretary," Oscar growled.

"And how was I supposed to get a hold of you?" Mr Fletcher groaned loudly. "Look, this isn't going to help us find her. We need to get back and figure out what to do. Maybe Amy will know where she's gone."

"She's got a landlady…"

"She cares too much about that old lady to put her in danger. What about that friend you told me about? Henry Lewis?"

Lottie felt lightheaded. They were going to go after Henry. She couldn't let that happen.

"I suppose she would go to him," Oscar mused. "She was always going to him even after I tried to shut him out. The bond between the two of them is incredibly strong; more than I thought."

"Then we'll go to his lodgings and wait for him to turn up. It'll be where we grab both." Mr Fletcher then walked away. "Then you're going to have to explain how she got away from us."

"Me? Why me?"

Oscar disappeared, and Lottie heard their voices fading away. Even after they were gone, and the silence was ringing in her ears, she couldn't move. She was scared if she tried, they would be there and would grab her. She lay in the dirt, slowly counting to one hundred, before she even thought about moving.

Henry was in danger as well. She had to get to him before Oscar and Mr Fletcher did. If she was lucky, she would get there first.

* * *

IT WAS dark by the time she reached the building where the paper was printed and where Henry worked. Lottie had been by a few times, but she had never been inside. She didn't even know if he was inside or not.

She had to find out, though. She couldn't stay outside when there was a chance Oscar and Mr Fletcher could grab her. If they were going to wait at his lodgings, they could come here as well. Lottie wasn't about to let Henry get hurt too.

She couldn't believe she had been taken in so easily by Oscar. He had been charming and kind towards her, showing the life that he lived and what could have been hers if she had married him. She had even developed feelings for him, but all the while he had been manipulating her so he could get her trapped to be kidnapped. He worked for the enemy, and it had almost worked. If she had agreed to marry him…

Maybe it was that thought at the back of her mind that had stopped her from accepting immediately. She had to have known, deep down, that he wasn't the right person for her. Something hadn't been right about him, although Lottie had done her best to ignore it. At the end of the day, though, it had been the reason she had hesitated on becoming Mrs Preston. Her gut instinct was saying it would be a bad idea.

And she was grateful for that. Otherwise, this would be turning out a lot worse than it already was.

Looking around, hoping that nobody was following her, she hurried across the road and into the newspaper's building. There was a porter in the lobby, sat behind a desk as he wrote in a huge ledger. He looked up as she entered.

"Yes, miss?"

"I'd like to see Henry Lewis, please," Lottie panted. "Is he in?"

"Who shall I say wants to see him?"

"My name's Lottie Watson."

The porter sat up.

"So, you're the Lottie we've been hearing about?"

"I beg your pardon?"

"He talks about you all the time. Won't stop, to the point we're getting sick of it." The man chuckled. "I don't think I've seen anyone so mad over another person. It's sweet and irritating at the same time."

Lottie didn't know what to say to that. She was still reeling from the fact Oscar had been in league with Mr Fletcher for years, and there was nothing left to react to the knowledge Henry had been talking about her so much to his colleagues. She ended up pacing around the lobby, trying to keep out of the way of the door. She was half-afraid that if she looked outside, Mr Fletcher would be there.

Had Amy managed to get away? How had they managed to force her to do this? Why hadn't Amy warned her? Those questions were going around in her head, and she couldn't stop them. It was too much for her.

Any minute now, she was going to wake up and find this was a bad dream. But she couldn't. This was very much real.

"Lottie?"

Henry appeared at the bottom of the stairs. He was in his shirtsleeves, which were rolled up above his elbows, and a smudge of something was on his face, his hair stuck up at odd angles. He looked like he had been sleeping at his desk.

It was the most relieving sight Lottie had ever seen in her life, and it made her burst into tears.

"Lottie!" Stunned, Henry hurried over and put his arms around her. "What's wrong? What happened?"

"It's...it's Oscar..." Lottie tried to speak through her tears. "He...he's in league...with Mr Fletcher."

"What?" Henry pushed her back enough to stare at her. "What are you saying?"

"He set me up." Lottie gulped, trying to get the air in. "He was a part of Mr Fletcher's...gang, or whatever you call it. They tried to trap me, but I got away..."

"I think you need to slow down." Henry put an arm around her shoulders and nodded at the porter. "Do you mind if we get a private room, Thomas?"

"Of course. Come with me."

Thomas led them into another part of the building and unlocked a room at the far end of the hall. It was simple, looking like an office that was barely used. Lottie looked around, noting how much it looked like a prison cell.

"Why is this place locked?" she asked.

"We work on the upper floors. These are for when we conduct interviews or talk to confidential informants so they're not walking around the building." Henry led her to the settee and sat them both down. "Now take a deep breath and start again. I want to know what you're talking about."

It took a moment, but Lottie managed to get her story out. She saw so many emotions pass across Henry's face, unable to grasp onto one of them. His eyes narrowed when she told him about Amy. Lottie wished she knew what was happening to Amy, but she was more focused on trying to keep Henry safe.

When she finished, Henry was silent for a moment. Then he stood and paced around the room, rubbing his hands over his face.

"Goodness, I can't believe this. That man was working with Fletcher, and they were working together to kidnap you again?"

"That's pretty much it." Lottie shifted on the settee. "I can't believe I fell for all of it. I thought someone liked me. He got me a good job and looked after me. All so he could get me to trust him."

"He was very good."

"I hesitated to agree to marry him," Lottie whispered, staring at the floor. "I couldn't bring myself to say yes, even after everything."

"That was your instincts telling you something wasn't right, and you've always listened to them." Henry sounded grim. "And it's a good thing you did this time, otherwise you might have vanished by now."

"He's coming after you. And Mrs Moore." Lottie felt the panic tighten in her chest. "I need to tell her about it. She needs to be safe."

"We can send her a message. She'll know what she needs to do to look after herself."

"But what about you?"

"I'll be focused on looking after you." Henry turned to her. "I'm not going to leave you alone, Lottie. I won't let that happen."

Lottie found her smiling at that. She could believe that Henry would do that. Unlike Oscar, he had always followed through on his promises. She could trust him.

"I feel like a complete fool for being taken in by him." She buried her head in her hands. "I should've listened to you in the beginning. I don't know why I didn't."

"You thought you knew what you were doing, and I was trusting you to make up your own mind." Henry approached her, crouching before her. He took her hands in his and gave her a smile. "I will always be around if you need me, Lottie. You know that. I'm not going anywhere."

"I know." Lottie rested her forehead against his. "You have no idea how grateful I am."

Her heart pounded as he reached up and touched her cheek. Then he pulled away abruptly, standing up and heading towards the door. Lottie swayed, almost falling off the settee. What had just happened?

"Anyway, there's something I need you to see, Lottie," Henry said gruffly. "I've got some information that I think you're going to like."

"I am?" She sat up. "What is it?"

"I know where your brother is."

He had barely finished before Lottie was jumping to her feet. "Really?"

"Yes. I've had it confirmed."

"Then take me to him." Lottie held up a hand as Henry started to speak. "No, don't start. I'm going to bring him back. It's the least I can do after abandoning him all these years."

Henry looked like he was going to argue. Then he sighed and nodded.

"All right. But we need to tread carefully. We could get into trouble if we get caught."

Lottie didn't care about that. She had to see her brother again.

CHAPTER 13

The factory was on the edge of the river, thick black smoke billowing out of the chimneys. It wasn't that far from the orphanage. Lottie remembered seeing the chimneys from the windows in her dormitory every day. This was where they put Billy?

He was this close, and she had never known.

The stench from the factory made her cough and her eyes water as she and Henry approached. They stood across the street from the main gates, and Henry pointed up at the huge building towering over them.

"I thought the best place to look first would be the immediate area. Fletcher wanted the girls, not the boys, so he would want to offload them as soon as he could."

"That makes sense," Lottie murmured.

"I've had a few people scouting the place, watching the workers coming and going. But the children had their own dormitories inside, so it's hard to find out if Billy's in there."

"Then how did you find out that he was? Did you go inside?"

"Didn't need to. We had a delivery of fine bone china to the shop next to the office, and I was coming back from lunch when I saw one of the boys helping with the delivery. He was older, but he looked a lot like Billy. Then I heard the man with the cart call him by name, and I just knew it was him."

"And you followed them back here?"

Henry nodded, giving her a smug look.

"I thought you would want to know as soon as possible. Once I finished my assignments, I was going to come by to tell you."

"When did you find out about this?" Lottie asked. "It wasn't a long time ago, was it?"

"It was earlier in the day, actually."

"What?" Lottie squealed, quieting down when Henry waved a hand at her. She lowered her voice to a loud whisper as a woman walked past giving her a strange look. "Why didn't you tell me then?"

"I had to be sure where he was. Then my editor told me to get on with my assignments, otherwise I'd have to work all night to get them out." Henry shook his head. "I was coming to see you as soon as I could, Lottie. It was only a few hours."

"But if Mr Fletcher put Billy here, he probably had someone come by to get him," she protested. "He could be gone…"

Her voice trailed away when she saw a cart trundling along the street. There was a large, broad-looking man sitting up front with the reins, grimy and with his face creased into a scowl. There were two boys sitting in the back, but Lottie couldn't see their faces. She pointed.

"Is that…?"

"That's the cart I saw and the same man," Henry said quietly, pulling her back. "Just wait. I want you to see if it is him."

Lottie wanted to rush forward and see if it was her brother, but Henry was right. If it wasn't him, she would have less chance of finding him. And she needed to be sure.

It had been years since she had seen him, and Lottie was scared that she wouldn't recognise him. Would she know him as soon as she laid eyes on him?

LOTTIE - THE RUNAWAY

The cart stopped across the street from them, and the boys jumped out. The one nearest them, as tall as Henry and thin, took off his cap and used it to rub his face. Lottie's breath hitched. There was no mistaking him. She was certain of that.

Pulling away from Henry, she stumbled towards him, slowing before she got too close. It felt like a dream. How was this possible? Was it really her brother? Lottie felt like she was going to break the spell and he would disappear, that this was all a dream.

Then he looked up and caught sight of her. He did a double-take, his jaw dropping and his eyes widening. She froze, her breath lodged in her chest as he moved towards her.

"Lottie?" he whispered. "Is that you?"

"Billy."

Lottie was lost for words. Her brother was right in front of her. She reached out and Billy immediately took her hand. He was real, and he was warm, his fingers rough under her touch.

She couldn't believe it.

"I...I can't believe it," she croaked. "You're really here."

"I was wondering if I'd see you again." Billy sounded like he was in a daze. "I thought you'd forgotten about me, though."

"No! I'd never forget about you." Lottie felt the tears building. "I missed you so much!"

"Billy!"

Billy looked back, and the man driving the cart was glaring at him.

"Get back inside! You shouldn't be flirting with young ladies!"

Billy glanced back at Lottie. She wanted to beg him to stay with her, but they would forcibly be parted again. An idea came to her. It was a dangerous one, and she shouldn't be thinking like that, but it was one way to get Billy out of there.

"What are you thinking?" Billy looked dubious. "I know that look. That's not changed in all this time."

"You think I'm planning something?"

"I know you are. What?"

123

Lottie's mind was racing, but she wasn't entirely sure if she could follow through. She wanted to take Billy away right now, to take him from his life. But that would cause a lot more trouble, and they would likely get caught. She couldn't do that to her brother, not after she literally just found him.

But then she thought about Oscar and Mr Fletcher. If they were the ones who put him in this place and knew that Lottie was close to finding him, there was a chance that Billy would be moved, and then she would have lost him for good. She couldn't let that happen.

"Billy, get back here!" The large man was approaching them with a scowl. "Get your hands off that girl and inside, otherwise I'm going to be having a few words with Mr Marston."

Billy tensed, and Lottie felt him clutch her hand tighter. That was enough for her to decide. She wasn't leaving him here.

"Run," she whispered.

"What?"

"We run. Now." Lottie looked back and saw Henry on the pavement, staring at them as if he knew she was going to do something drastic. "Just stay close to me and we get out of here."

Billy's eyes widened.

"But...where will we go? What if...?"

"Don't argue! Come on!"

Lottie tugged at him, hoping that would be enough for him to start running. Thankfully, Billy caught himself before he stumbled off his feet and began to follow her.

"Get back here!" The man bellowed, charging after them. "You little harlot! Get your hands off him!"

"Lottie!" Henry shouted, hurrying after them.

But he was too far away as Lottie ducked into an alley, Billy following her.

* * *

LOTTIE - THE RUNAWAY

They ran down the narrow path, Lottie eventually letting go of Billy's hand as she tried to keep her balance. It had been a long time since she had run holding onto someone, and it felt as if she was going to fall over.

The alley turned into a lot of twists and turns, and soon Lottie was lost. She had no idea where she was going, and she was beginning to panic that they were going to come back to where they started, and she didn't want to run into that man again.

"We need to slow down," Billy panted, grabbing at her sleeve. "I…I can't breathe…"

"We can't stop." Although Lottie did slow to a quick walk, looking both ways at the end of the alley before taking the left route. "We've got to get out of here. If we get caught, there's a chance I'll be dragged in there as well. Especially once Mr Fletcher finds out what I'm doing."

"Mr Fletcher?" Billy tightened his grip on her wrist, making her stop. "What are you talking about?"

"He's the one who put you in there, right?" Lottie turned to her brother, tilting her head back to look up at him. How had he gotten so much taller than her? "You've been here since I left the orphanage, right? It was because of him."

Billy stared at her in alarm.

"He's the one who did this? But I didn't know!"

"How were you supposed to know? It's not as if he's going to tell you!"

"How did you find out about it, though?"

Lottie took a deep breath.

"It's a long story. Which I'll tell you once we get away from here. I've got somewhere we can go, and Henry can use his contacts…"

"Wait, Henry? As in Henry the printer's apprentice?"

"He's here as well. He helped me find you."

And now Lottie had no idea where he was. They had acted on impulse, and now they had lost Henry. Lottie hoped that they would meet up again shortly, and that Henry wouldn't be angry with him. Right now, they needed to find a way out of the twists and turns they were stuck in.

She squeezed Billy's hands.

"I'll answer any questions you have when we get out of here. But first, we need to run. You don't want to go back there, do you?"

"Of course not!" Billy's answer was adamant. "I hate it there. They beat the children for breathing the wrong way. And I can't remember the last time I slept properly. We never seem to rest. I don't want to go back there."

"Then you'll come with me and we'll talk later. I promise."

Billy looked uncertain, and Lottie wished she could go back to the children they used to be. There was a shadow of pain behind Billy's eyes that made her want to cry. He shouldn't have gone through that. Up until they were separated, she had done whatever she could to keep the pain away and to protect him. And she had failed.

Not again. It wasn't happening anymore.

Finally, Billy nodded and straightened up.

"All right. Let's go. But I'm so tired, I don't think I can keep up for much longer."

Lottie hoped that wouldn't be the case. Beckoning him to follow her, they reached the end of the alley and found it opened onto a main street. Looking up and down, it didn't seem like they were going to be noticed. There was no sign of the man who had been chasing them, and Lottie couldn't see Oscar or Mr Fletcher.

"Let's get moving." Lottie took her brother's hand. "We'll be out of here soon. Then Mrs Moore will look after you."

"Who's Mrs Moore?"

"A godsend. You'll like her."

"And how did you end up meeting Henry again?"

Lottie was about to tell him when she saw two familiar figures appear at the end of the road. It was Oscar and Mr

Fletcher. They were walking quickly along the street in deep conversation between themselves. For now, they hadn't seen them, but they would soon be running into them.

Lottie began to panic. She could run across the street and walk there, but if Oscar caught sight of them, he wouldn't be quiet about it. And Mr Fletcher would then give chase. They would have to keep running.

She looked around. What could they do? They needed to do something. Maybe go back into the alley again?

The rumbling of a carriage reached her ears, deafening her as it pulled up alongside her. Then the door opened, and Henry leaned out.

"Get in!" he demanded. "Quickly!"

Lottie wasn't about to be told twice. She pushed Billy inside and was about to follow him when she felt eyes on her. Looking around, she saw Oscar staring at her. It sent a shiver down her spine. She barely recognised him now. He looked like a monster, his eyes narrowed, and his face fixed into an angry scowl.

How could she have been taken in by him?

"Lottie!" Henry grabbed her arm and pulled. "Get in!"

Tearing her eyes away from Oscar, Lottie allowed herself to be yanked into the carriage, sprawling across the seat as Henry shut the door and the carriage started off again. She was aware of someone shouting and then slapping the side of the carriage, but they didn't stop. Lottie half-expected the door to be pulled open and Oscar or Mr Fletcher would reach in to drag her and Billy out.

But it didn't happen. The banging soon stopped, and the carriage turned, throwing Lottie against Henry. Pushing herself away, she opened the blind of the window and looked out. She could see Oscar and Mr Fletcher get to the corner of the street, staring after the carriage as it hurried away.

That had been so close, and the knowledge they were almost caught again opened the gates. Lottie couldn't help herself.

She slumped on the seat, leaning against Henry as he put his arms around her. Then she burst into tears. Henry rocked her, holding her tightly.

"It's all right, Lottie." His voice was gentle over the loud rumbling of the carriage. "I've got you. You're safe now."

Lottie knew that. But it didn't make her feel any better. Not right now.

CHAPTER 14

When Lottie opened her eyes, she found herself staring at the ceiling. For a moment, she wondered where she was. Then she realised she was in her bedroom, and the sun was peeking through the thin curtains.

How had she ended up here? The last thing Lottie remembered was crying in Henry's arms. Had she passed out and he took her home?

And where was Billy?

Lottie sat up. What had happened to her brother? Was he with her? Henry had to have brought him here as well. It would be ridiculous if she got Billy away, only for Henry to throw him aside.

A knock at the door didn't help to soothe her panic.

"Come in."

The door opened, and Billy stuck his head into the room. He gave her a smile.

"You're awake."

"Billy!" Lottie's panic dissipated. "Thank God! I was beginning to wonder where you were."

"Mrs Moore said I could sleep on the settee in the living room. I've had a wash and had something to eat." Billy entered the room and closed the door behind him. "She's nice. A little strange, but she's very nice."

"She is." Lottie smiled. "I was very lucky meeting her when I did."

They stared at each other. Then Billy rushed towards her, flinging his arms around her. Lottie gasped as she was knocked backwards onto the bed.

"Careful!" she gasped. "You're bigger than me now!"

"Oh, sorry!" Billy shifted back, allowing her to sit up. "I forgot. I missed you so much."

"I missed you, too." Lottie hugged him again. "I thought I'd never see you again. I wish you'd come with me."

"You were always protecting me until then. I wanted to be that one who protected you."

Lottie tried not to cry at that. Her little brother had been looking out for her, and she had worried herself sick over him.

"Henry told me what happened. About how you met again, and how you managed to make a good life for yourself." Billy paused, pulling back and giving her an apprehensive look. "I also know about Oscar Preston, and how he was working with Mr Fletcher on…well, you know…and how they were trying…"

"I don't want to think about that," Lottie cut him off, trying not to sound snappish. She felt like she was going to be sick knowing that she had almost gotten herself back into the mess she had run away from. "I was lucky and managed to get away. If I hadn't gotten you out of there when I did…"

"They would have kept us apart for longer, maybe forever." Billy shook his head. "They're disgusting people, using others to get the money they want to make themselves rich. I can't believe they were watching you and trying to get you back for their own selfish gains."

LOTTIE - THE RUNAWAY

"I can't believe I almost fell for it as well." Lottie felt ashamed telling her little brother about it. She drew her knees up and hugged them to her chest. "Oscar was so charming. I thought he was genuinely interested in me. But then I found that letter from Mr Fletcher, and I…"

"He was gaining your trust and doing well at it as well." Billy sounded grim. "But he didn't anticipate you being so clever. You've always been able to tell if someone's good or bad."

"I failed when it came to Oscar."

"You were a little slow on the uptake there."

Lottie managed a small smile with that. Billy leaned into her, resting his forehead against hers.

"I've missed you, sister. I'm glad I've found you again."

"And I'm relieved I got to you before they did." Lottie sat back. "Now we've got to figure out what to do with you. I know Mrs Moore will help you if you give back."

Billy chuckled.

"We've already had a conversation about that. She said that she's more than happy to find good employment for me, but I've got to work hard and make sure I pay rent once I turn eighteen. And I need to have some lessons to make sure I keep up with my education." He made a face at that. "I'm not looking forward to that part. I haven't had any lessons since I moved into that factory. I can't remember the last time I read a book."

"It's not that difficult to get back into it. And you'll have more opportunities when you're older, so it works in your favour." Lottie nudged him off the bed before getting off the mattress. "Where's Mrs Moore now?"

"She's gone to ask around a few friends of hers."

"She's gone out." Lottie stared. "But Oscar and Mr Fletcher know where we live! If she's seen by them…"

"I don't think you have to worry about that."

"How can you say that?"

Billy grinned.

"You can talk to Henry about it. He's downstairs right now."

Lottie had almost forgotten about him, being overjoyed at knowing her brother was finally back with her.

"Henry? What could he have done?"

"He can tell you himself. Although he looks like he's been up all night, so he might fall asleep while talking to you."

"All night." Lottie frowned. "How long have I been asleep?"

"You and I ran away from the factory yesterday afternoon. It's mid-morning."

She had been asleep for that long? Lottie couldn't believe it. She had never done that before. Billy gave Lottie's bed a longing look.

"I know I've already slept, but I'm still so tired. Do you mind...?"

"Of course not. Make yourself at home." Lottie squeezed his hand. "Make the most of it. You deserve it."

With a relieved smile, Billy clambered into the bed, pulling the sheets up almost to his nose. Lottie wondered if the bed in the factory had been comfortable. Probably not, they didn't care about anyone's comfort at night if they had somewhere to sleep. This was likely the first time he had a bed to himself without having to share it.

Washing quickly and changing into a clean dress, Lottie slipped out of the room. Billy was snoring by the time he shut the door, which made Lottie smile. Some things never changed.

Henry was in the sitting room, staring out of the window as Lottie entered. His hair was standing on end, and he had taken off his jacket. When he turned to look at her, Lottie could see the pale complexion and the dark circles under his eyes. He had certainly not had much sleep, if he had managed to lie down at all.

"What happened to you?" Lottie approached him. "Have you rested at all?"

"Not really. I've been up all night."

"What? Why?"

"Getting things sorted." Henry gestured towards the settee. "How are you feeling? You passed out in my arms after you stopped crying. I think you were so exhausted that you just... well..."

"I can't remember anything after, so that makes sense." Lottie looked at the clock, but the time didn't make much sense to her. "Have I really been asleep for such a long time?"

"Yes. After everything that happened, I'm not surprised. You needed it."

"And what have you been up to? Why have you been up all night?"

"A lot of things had to be done." Henry paused. "I went to go and see Amy first. After what you said about her..."

"Amy." Lottie had practically forgotten about her. "How is she? What happened to her?"

"She's shaken, but she says she can cope as long as you're out of their clutches."

"Why were Mr Fletcher and Oscar using her?"

"Well, you wouldn't have left your house to go somewhere if it had been them asking you to, but you trusted Amy. She said she wrote the letter under duress, and when you arrived, she wanted you to run." Henry rubbed his eyes and yawned. "You have no idea the relief that came from her when I told her you got away and found Billy as well. I thought she was going to cry."

"And they didn't hurt her too much?"

"The bruises will go down, and she's going to be a bit more reclusive for now, but I managed to get her to talk to the constables. They listened and went out to arrest Preston and Fletcher."

Lottie was in a daze with this. She had contemplated going to the constables before, but with the contacts Oscar had, she didn't think he would be arrested, or he would have someone get him out before he even got charged with anything. Those with power were treated differently, and Lottie hated it.

"Have they found them?" she asked. "And do you think they'll be able to make the charges stick?"

"If they don't, their reputations will be ruined regardless."

"How is that…?"

Henry grinned.

"That's why I was up all night. I was in long talks with my employer about what happened. Apparently, this problem of girls disappearing around London has been ongoing for a long time, and while my other journalists had a few leads they were never able to get anywhere. Nobody knew who was involved in it, either."

Lottie could see where this was going.

"But you found who was a part of it," she murmured. "You told them about Oscar."

"Well, to tell you the truth, Lottie…" Henry cleared his throat. "I've been investigating him for a while."

"What?"

"I suspected that something wasn't quite right about him. He set my own instincts off, telling me he was bad news." His face flushed and he glanced away. "I will admit most of it was spurred on by the fact he was making your head turn and I didn't want that to happen. I was trying to find something to make him back off."

"And you found something."

"It was a complete accident, and I wasn't anticipating it. When I saw him exchanging money with someone and girls were taken out of his carriage before being pushed into a building, I knew he was up to something nefarious." Henry shifted uncomfortably. "I wish I'd told you before about this but given how affected you were by him I didn't want you to think I was telling lies to get you to turn your back on him. If I tried, I figured you would be driven further into his arms."

Lottie started to protest that she wouldn't have done that, that she would have believed him, but then she remembered how she had behaved when Oscar first started paying her attention. And she knew that Henry was right; she wouldn't have believed him and would have accused him of being jealous.

Sighing, she pinched the bridge of her nose.

"Did you notify anyone about the girls?"

"I did, but there wasn't much to go on, and I had a feeling the constables wouldn't give it too much focus. These people were good at keeping out of trouble. So, I had to be a bit cleverer with how I collected evidence." Henry shrugged. "I work for the newspaper, after all. All I need to do is have facts that had been checked and checked again that I could publish, and then when there is an uproar the constables would have to investigate."

"Using the paper to make people aware of what was happening," Lottie said quietly.

"It's been done before. Even if there is no proof of someone being involved, public opinion is very strong. You just need to give it the slightest suggestion, and people will run with it. It can make a reputation crumble within hours, and I'm sure you've seen it happen in the past."

She had. She hadn't witnessed it personally, but she had more than once read something scandalous in the paper and it had ended up ruining someone. Even if it came out that they were an innocent party in the scandal, it didn't matter if public opinion had already made up its mind. If that happened to Oscar, he wouldn't be able to cope with it. Everyone's eyes were going to be on him no matter what he did, and the constables would be aware of him. It would be rather hard to do anything when people were watching him. Oscar didn't know the scrutiny. Lottie knew he would struggle to cope under that sort of pressure.

And that was if he wasn't arrested and put in prison. She hoped that would happen.

"So, you've printed that in the paper?" she asked. "You've taken a shot at him?"

"Over what he was witnessed doing, what he did to you, and what he planned to do with your brother should his original plan not work. Fletcher's been mentioned as well, and I've made sure all the details are plentiful and easy to check." Henry spread his hands. "Anything I could think of to make sure they knew if they tried coming anywhere near you, it would be noticed."

"And you think it's going to be that easy for them to keep away?"

"We'll find out if it actually works soon."

Lottie's head was spinning. It felt like Henry had been more productive than her recently. Standing up, she went over to the window and stared out at the park across the street. There were children playing on the grass, and she could hear their laughter through the closed window. She wished she'd had a childhood like that in her past. Instead, she and Billy had been unable to have any happiness once their parents died. They were thrown into the orphanage by their aunt and left to be forgotten about.

A part of her wondered where her aunt was now, but she didn't want to think about her. That wasn't going to make her feel any better. The woman was dead, as far as she was concerned.

"I'm stunned that you've done all of that for me," she said to Henry. "I didn't expect any of it."

"Why wouldn't you believe I'd do that for you?"

"Well, we're friends...I mean..."

She heard Henry get to his feet and his footsteps moved closer to her. Then he touched her shoulder, urging her to turn around.

"Do you think I was really doing this because I see you as a friend, Lottie?"

"I don't..."

"You haven't figured out how I feel about you all this time? I love you. I have done for a long time. The thought of having you being under this man's thumb scared and angered me. He had so much planned for you, and you wouldn't have agreed to any of it." Henry swallowed. "I remember what happened to you before, and there was no chance I was going to walk away from any of it. You needed someone on your side, someone to rescue you."

Lottie didn't know what to say to that. She didn't want to start crying again. She reached out and pressed her hands on his chest. Henry's arms went around her, and he kissed her forehead.

"I know this might not be the right time for me to ask, especially after what's happened to you, but I want you to know that I'm never going anywhere. I love you, and I'm always going to be there if you need me."

"I know." Lottie looked up at him and smiled. "I've known since we met that you were always going to be there. And I'll forever remember that."

"And what about Preston?"

She hoped never to hear his name again. This time, Lottie was going to embrace her initial feelings. She rose up on tiptoe and kissed him.

"I was beginning to pull away from him once I found out about Mr Fletcher. What I thought I felt about him was just an idea. It was built on a false promise. But with you…" She touched his cheek. "You've been honest with me since the beginning. You've made it clear how you feel, and you've never turned your back on me. I loved you for it, and I feel awful for dismissing it when I had my attention taken for a while."

Henry blinked.

"Loved? As in the past?"

"And the present. Let me try again." Lottie kissed him again. "I love you, too. I think I always have, and it took until recently to realise it. I'm sorry I'm slow on the uptake."

Henry laughed, wrapping his arms tightly around her.

"I'm used to it. I wasn't going to push you on anything,

although you did scare me when you were spending a lot of time with Preston."

"Well, that's not going to happen anymore." Lottie hugged him. "I know where I need to be."

Henry groaned, rocking her as they embraced.

"And I know where that is. Right here with me."

Lottie couldn't agree more with that statement.

EPILOGUE

1875

"I'm just going out, Lottie," Billy said as he headed towards the door. "I'll be back later."

Lottie looked up and frowned.

"Where are you going, Billy? You're not going back into work, are you?"

"Of course not. I'm not back at work until the morning." Billy blushed. "It's just that I'm going to see Maisie Meadows. She and I…well…"

Lottie caught on quickly. Her brother was going out with a girl. Part of her wanted to tell him not to go, but she knew she couldn't tell him what to do. He was almost eighteen, and far bigger than her. She needed to stop being a mother to him. She smiled at him, reaching for a cloth to wipe her ink-stained hands.

"You two have fun. Make sure you make the most of it. The weather's lovely today, so it should be nice later this evening."

"All right," Billy mumbled. "Bye."

He hurried out, and Lottie heard Henry chuckled from across the room. He looked up from his desk, his eyes twinkling.

"Early love. It's adorable, isn't it?"

"It feels so strange that Billy is now courting girls. It didn't seem that long ago that he was still a child."

"You missed out on several years of his life through no fault of your own," Henry pointed out. "It's going to take some adjusting. Just trust his judgement and don't restrict him too much, and things will be fine."

Lottie knew that, but it was easier said than done. She didn't want to push her brother away because she was too busy mothering him. This was a time when she needed to listen to her husband's wise words.

Husband. That felt like a dream, even after almost two years of marriage. And it still made her smile.

It was in the late autumn that they got married with just Mrs Moore, Amy, and Billy as witnesses, not wanting to make a big affair of it. Mrs Moore had been more than happy to help them with anything, and after asking around her many friends and acquaintances, she was able to find them a good home to live in and Lottie got a job at the nearby printing shop.

Henry, still at the newspaper, came by every day and struck up a friendship with the owner, who was close to retirement and had been worried about his business once he was gone. So, Henry had made him a deal that he couldn't refuse. Now the old owner was living in Cornwall, enjoying his retirement with his family, and Henry now owned the printing shop that Lottie worked at. They got to work side by side every day, which had made Lottie worried in the beginning. She was scared they would start arguing all the time and begin to hate each other.

But it had worked out. Somehow, they were still in love despite working with each other every day and going to sleep at night without any major squabble. It was surprisingly quite nice, and Lottie loved it.

She was about to get back to the printing when she heard a babble and something nudged into the back of her leg. Looking down, she saw her daughter Daisy clutching onto her skirt with a toothy grin.

"Mama," she chattered, shaking Lottie's skirt.

"You're awake now, are you?" Lottie wiped her hands on her apron and picked up her daughter. "I thought you'd be sleeping for a little longer."

"I don't think she knows how to sleep anymore," Henry remarked. "She's constantly jumping on our bed and then climbing in to sleep. She has her own cot."

"She just wants to be close to us, that's all."

"And one of us is going to be sleeping in the cot if she keeps using her elbows and knees while she sleeps," her husband grumbled.

Lottie laughed, kissing Daisy's cheek before carrying her over to Henry. He put his pen down and rubbed his eyes, clearly exhausted, but he smiled lovingly at his daughter as Lottie put Daisy in his lap. Daisy giggled and patted his chest with a thumping hand.

"Papa!"

"Yes, I'm papa." Henry kissed her head and held onto her as she balanced on his lap. "And you're going to get in the way, aren't you? How about we go for a walk to the park? See if you want to count the ducks in the pond."

Daisy squealed, which made Lottie laugh. Their daughter loved the ducks.

"Do you want me to come with you?"

"No, we've still got some things to finish off here." Henry stood, picking up his daughter and holding her on his hip. "Besides, you can use this to have a bit of time to yourself."

"Are you sure?"

"I can look after her. Daisy's no problem." Henry kissed her before he stepped around his wife. "We won't be long. I'm sure Daisy's going to be hungry, though, so I might take her to Mrs Moore to have an afternoon playing so we can finish here."

Lottie smiled.

"She's really throwing herself into the role of a grandmother, isn't she?"

"I don't think we can blame her. She's certainly taken us in as family."

Lottie couldn't argue with that. With a kiss on her daughter's head, she watched her family leave the shop. Then she was on her own. It was a quiet day, and their only employee, a young lad named Jonathan, was off on an errand. For now, Lottie was on her own.

Not something she got nowadays, and she thrived on it.

She turned away from the desk, only to catch sight of an article in the newspaper, folded on top of the other paperwork. Henry had brought it in earlier but neither of them had read it. Curious, Lottie picked it up and unfolded it.

It was about Oscar. He had vanished from London after more evidence came to light that he was a part of a bigger group kidnapping girls and selling them into slavery or other horrible jobs, either in England or abroad. He was one of those further up the hierarchy, and when his house was being searched he vanished. Lottie hadn't heard from him in two years.

Now the news was saying he had been found and apprehended in Holland. They were bringing him back to England for his trial, and he wasn't likely to see daylight for a long time if things went as they should.

Lottie felt the relief flood through her. Mr Fletcher had been found and arrested years ago, and he was already in prison for his actions. Now Oscar was caught. She could stop looking over her shoulder, wondering if he was going to turn up again.

She was free. For the first time in years, she felt truly free. It felt like a lot of weight had come off her shoulders.

Beaming, Lottie put the paper down and went back to her work. Maybe she should suggest to Henry that they go out to dinner tonight, just the two of them. Then she could really celebrate knowing that her past was well and truly put behind her.

The End

If you enjoyed this story, could I please ask you to leave a review on Amazon?

Thank you so much.

Printed in Dunstable, United Kingdom